ALSO BY STACEY GOLDBLATT

Stray

STACEY GOLDBLATT

DELACORTE PRESS

All rights reserved. Published in the United States by Delacorte Press, an imprint of Random House Children's Books, a division of Random House, Inc., New York.

Delacorte Press is a registered trademark and the colophon is a trademark of Random House, Inc.

Visit us on the Web! www.randomhouse.com/teens
Educators and librarians, for a variety of teaching tools,
visit us at www.randomhouse.com/teachers

Library of Congress Cataloging-in-Publication Data

Goldblatt, Stacey.
Girl to the core / Stacey Goldblatt. — 1st ed.
p. cm.
Summary: Fifteen-year-old Molly gains support from her extended Irish American family and enlightenment in Girl Corps philosophy and activities as she deals with a cheating boyfriend and an overbearing best friend.
ISBN: 978-0-385-73609-1 (trade) ISBN: 978-0-385-90587-9 (lib. bdg.)
ISBN: 978-0-375-89105-2 (e-book) [1. Self-respect—Fiction. 2. Dating (Social customs)—Fiction. 3. Loss (Psychology)—Fiction. 4. Irish Americans—Fiction. 5. Family life—California—Fiction. 6. Accordion—Fiction. 7. Californian, Southern—Fiction.]
PZ7.G56449 Gir 2009   [Fic]—dc22   2008032350

The text of this book is set in 11.75-point Baskerville.
Book design by Vikki Sheatsley
Printed in the United States of America
10 9 8 7 6 5 4 3 2 1
First Edition

For Mom, Mindy, and Eve,
who helped this girl find her core

ACKNOWLEDGMENTS

Gratitude and thanks to:

Maria Bertrand, Beth Brust, Kim Douillard, Kathleen Gallagher, Jeremy Goldblatt, Jayne Haines, Sara Hansen, Joan Kelch, Danan MacNamara, Al Mooney, and Cheryl and John Ritter for honest feedback.

The music and poetry of Paddy Carty, the Celtic Fiddle Festival, Patti Furlong, Leanne Harte, Flogging Molly, Van Morrison, the Pogues, Thin Lizzy, and the Young Dubliners.

The team of people at Random House: Beverly Horowitz, Kathy Dunn, Abigail Powers, Colleen Fellingham, Barbara Perris, and the others who make books out of stories and put them into the hands of readers.

Steven Chudney for his support and the wherewithal to make things happen.

Claudia Gabel, who shaped and guided this novel with expertise, patience, and trust.

Girls everywhere who continue to search and redefine what it means to be a female in a world that's all too eager to do it for them.

GIRL
TO THE
CORE

Clay with trapped air will explode in the kiln, so I hit the slab in front of me, which—I tell you true—resembles a giant hunk of turd. Gross, but I'm not artistic. In fact, the poor mound appears worse than when I started at the beginning of the period.

"Focus, Molly," Ms. Pinkwater says from the glazing station across the broiling hot ceramics room. "You're slapping it." She punches a fist in the air above her shaggy gray hair; a bracelet that looks like a couch spring clutches her arm. "Use force. *Pound* it."

Standing behind me, Trevor laughs.

"Shut up," I say jokingly, and point to the poster on the wall of the lily-white statue man who, according to Ms. Pinkwater's introduction to classic sculpture, is famous. "I'm not a David, like you."

Trevor swipes his glistening forehead with the back

of his hand. "Mol, David is the name of the *sculpture*. Michelangelo is the artist."

I'm such an idiot. I can't even joke around right.

Beads of sweat trickle around my neck, underneath my unenchanted forest of red hair. "It's too hot for art," I say. Trevor's dimple puckers.

I swear that dimple is like a separate part of him. In the three months we've been a couple I've even had the urge to name the dimple, but *Seventeen* magazine says boyfriends hate baby talk, and I suspect naming a dimple might qualify. Trevor's got California-grown good looks—brown eyes that flicker with confidence, a muscular copper-toned body, and dark hair flecked with golden highlights. Every inch of him appears as if he's been double-dipped in sunshine. Still, it's that dimple puckered in his right cheek that gets me every time.

"Here, let me do it," he offers with a quick glance at Ms. Pinkwater, who mimes brushstroke technique to a pod of students. As the sole Advanced Ceramics student in the room, Trevor can advise us beginners, but he's not supposed to actually do the work for us.

I lean closer to his ear, where a small silver hoop earring dangles. I love that he's both manly and artsy. "Thanks, Michelangelo."

Trevor pummels my clay, while I become a shallow, gawky girl intensely distracted by the ripples along his gleaming forearm. "See? You just keep at it."

"Easy for you to say." Suddenly, this feels like a conversation beneath the actual conversation. Like he's giving me a motivational speech: If I *just keep at it*, I won't stomp on the brakes every time we make out.

This does not mean that I'm a quitter. Even with a spastic hand cramp I can twiddle through "The Tiny Trooper" on my button accordion as if I'm possessed by Paddy O'Brien himself. It's only when it comes to Trevor—and clay—that I lack the initiative.

"Molly." Guesstimating from the proximity of Ms. Pinkwater's disappointed voice, she's about a foot behind me.

I turn and see that I've miscalculated—she's a few inches away from my face. Her eyebrows dip with the weight of disappointment. "This is *art*. No one can do it for you."

Trevor jumps in. "I was only—"

"Shh." Ms. Pinkwater cuts him off, her palm softly raised.

"I'm sorry, Ms. Pinkwater," I say.

"There are no apologies in art." Ms. Pinkwater turns to Trevor. "Go on over to Nicole at the wheel. Help her with the foot pedal. Hands off her clay, got it, Trev?"

"Gotcha," he says with a shy nod.

I should have stuck to my guns in August when I hesitantly agreed to change my class schedule at Trevor's nudging: from environmental science to ceramics. He figured it was the only way we could have a class together, him being a junior and me being a sophomore this year. Even though I love being with

Trevor, I think my place is more with cumulonimbus clouds and flower pollination than clay lumps.

Ms. Pinkwater peers at me. With her tall frame, scraggly hair, and gauzy dresses, she looks like what I envision the Celtic goddesses to be in the bedtime stories Daddy used to tell me when I was a little girl. I wouldn't be surprised if her unicorn stood in the staff parking lot next to Mr. Benton's corn-powered golf cart. "Art requires observation and imagination, Molly."

Just my poor luck that I've got imagination deficit disorder. "I'm not very imaginative."

She inhales deeply and exhales dramatically. "Some artists know what they're going to create before they start, some have to find it. Trust your artistic intuition."

Coincidentally, I don't have that, either. "But—"

"Intuition, Molly. *Feel* it." She walks away, backward, toward the glazing station. "Create your own vision."

Speaking of vision, I behold Trevor standing next to Nicole Lightfoot, who struggles with her own wet clump on the ceramic wheel. I can hardly blame her when she blushes as she notices Trevor standing beside her.

After all, I spent most of last year in PE biting my lip as I watched Trevor and his miraculous body sprint, dribble, and breaststroke. He was so at ease. So self-assured. And very much an unattainable sophomore, with Felicia Mitchell as his girlfriend. Of course, just because he had a girlfriend didn't mean I couldn't dream about him or smile back when he looked at me.

I was simply thankful he didn't recognize me as the bespectacled accordionist from elementary school who crawled a grade behind him each year, wishing that one day he'd anoint her with a personal "hello."

I assumed he didn't, because at the beginning of second semester last year, when my PE teacher put us together as tennis partners, Trevor and I became good friends. We started hanging out together after school at Heritage Park, where he and some of his buddies slacklined. Apparently, Felicia was too cool to walk across a thick, nylon line anchored between two trees. I don't know who suffered more, me, for falling on my butt hundreds of times because I have the balance of a drunkard, or Felicia, who lost her grip on Trevor while I kept bouncing like a circus monkey from the flexible slackline into his arms.

On the night of our first kiss—which happened the day after he broke up with Felicia—Trevor told me that he loved how easygoing I was.

Except I'm not sure that still holds true, because the past couple of weeks he has wanted to do more than just kiss me. I'm learning that holding Trevor off is just as difficult as slacklining, if not harder. At least when I slacklined I knew a wobble would cost me only a two-foot fall. With Trevor, I'm not sure how much distance there is between me continuing to say no and a breakup.

Ms. Pinkwater tings her five-minute-warning chime

on her Tibetan singing bowl and snaps me to attention. As we clean up our workspaces, she mentions she has a singing bowl at home that she uses to center her chakras. I don't exactly know what a chakra is, but I think I have one somewhere inside me, because each time she taps that thing all the stress from being ceramically impaired vanishes with the realization that in five minutes, I'll have Trevor all to myself.

My excitement turns to panic. In less than a half hour we'll be on his living room couch, where on Tuesday, he planted soft kisses along my face and yesterday, he told me, "I want you." I'm nervous about where this will lead and what will happen if I don't follow.

This morning, while driving me to school in her little blue tin-can car, my best friend, Vanessa, who's definitely more than a few steps ahead of me in all things boy, laid out the "unspoken" rule. "Molly, Trevor has . . . a *past* with Felicia. You know what that *means*, don't you?"

"He's not pressuring me, Nessa."

"Whatever. Just know you're the next notch in his belt, sugar cube."

I try to shake off Vanessa's warning and moisten my heart-shaped brown clump with a wet sponge. Then I wrap it inside its plastic bag, strip off Daddy's old oversized button-up shirt smock, and stuff it all inside my cubby.

Over at the sink, underneath the sign that reads NEVER HANDLE ANOTHER PERSON'S WORK, EVEN IF IT

LOOKS COOL!, Trevor and I share the faucet. He rubs my hands under the water. "Sorry about helping you."

"No apologies in art, remember?"

Dimple alert. "I do have a surprise to show you," he says.

"I have one for you, too." I flick him with soapy bubbles.

He reels back. "Well, forget it now!"

I grab a paper towel and dab the water spots on his face. "*Pleeeze* show me!"

He gazes over at Ms. Pinkwater, who is busy helping someone scrape a warped vase off the potter's wheel and probably reciting some more art teacher incantations. Trevor takes my hand. "Over here." We slip away as the rest of the class finishes wiping down tabletops and cleaning up at the sinks.

Trevor leads me to the open, cooled-off kiln, where scattered projects shine with their new coat of cooked glaze. Strangely, the kiln feels a lot cooler than the rest of the ceramics room. A disheveled Justin Kubilnicky lifts a deformed little plate off the top shelf. He looks from Trevor to me and back again. "I was just leaving."

Trevor waits until Justin's gone. "Close your eyes." I do. He lifts my hands and places something heavy there. "Guess what it is."

It's round with a concave underside, smooth to the touch. The surface is bumpy and uneven. "Is it a ceramic hubcap?"

"Smart-ass. Just open your eyes."

In my hands is a mask sculpted with a face that resembles mine. Its glazed coils of rust-colored hair poke out in all directions, like rays of the sun. The other features are simple: almond-shaped green eyes, bubbly pink lips. I'm somewhat offended at the fact that Trevor perceives me in a bad-hair-day light, but at the same time, this is from him. He made it. For me. It's so . . . sweet!

I hug the mask in my arm, corner Trevor, and touch my lips to his. Warmth rolls over my shoulders as our mouths meld, and every worry in my head drifts away—ooh, now I think I know where my chakra might be.

After school, Trevor and I pad across Hilldale High's treeless parking lot toward his Jeep, the heat from the asphalt seeping up to my ankles as if hell's cauldron burbles directly below us.

You'd think most people in the parking lot would duck into their cars to make a quick getaway from school, but ours is an asphalt Mecca of social mingling. Even the nondrivers stick around here as long as they can until Chuck and Gerald, our bicycle-riding security Gestapo, threaten detention hall.

Trevor squeezes my hand. "I liked that."

"Liked what?" I ask.

"That you took charge back there in the kiln." His eyebrows jig.

Blood rushes to my face with the force of a wildfire. I hate that I blush. Urgh! The curse of being fair-skinned. I'm like a walking mood ring.

I smile at him, although I don't think anyone, especially Vanessa, sees me as the take-charge type.

I spot the spare tire on the swing-gate of the shiny red Jeep Trevor's parents gave him on his sixteenth birthday, when Felicia Mitchell was riding passenger side. I still can't get over the fact that now *I'm* the girl who gets to sit shotgun.

Last year, I'd watch Trevor and Felicia leave school together. It was as if my next-door neighbor, Claire, whose closet looks like a Barbie doll landfill, had plopped a life-sized Barbie and Ken into Trevor's Jeep. They looked perfect together. Her flowy blond, his clean-cut brunet. Except now, Barbie's been replaced by me, some redheaded knock-off dollar-store Barbie who doesn't move fast like Felicia.

I let go of Trevor's hand to get into the car, but the sudden thought of Felicia propels me toward him again. I kiss his warm lips, confirming that this is for real. "Mmm," Trevor says.

I don't know what's gotten into me! I pull back. I'm so flushed that my face must be Hot Tamale red. He whispers, "You're so spontaneous today." When he lets go, a nervous laugh escapes me.

Spontaneous. Right. My life is as predictable as the weekly entertainment schedule over at my aunt Tipper's pub, the Banshee's Wake. Which reminds me, I need to be there early tonight for Granddad's seventy-eighth birthday celebration. Daddy, the uncles, and I are going to play him a special set.

I climb into the vinyl bucket seat, thankful that Trevor keeps towels slung over them to prevent butt burn. Trevor buckles his seat belt. "You coming over to my house?"

"I've got to be at the Banshee by five. Why don't we just hang out at my house today?"

"My house is closer." He doesn't want to come over. "I can still drop you off by five."

"Sure." I'm such a wimp. We really should be at my house sometimes so that he can get to know my family. It's not a good sign that Daddy still calls him *that boy*.

Trevor jiggles the stick shift and we begin our exit from the parking lot, a slow crawl deadened by speed bumps that cause the Jeep, and my boobs, to bounce.

It makes sense that he'd rather be at his house. When we hooked up in June, I preferred being at his house, too. There's rarely a sign of parental supervision; his folks are workaholic attorneys. We spent a lot of time there this summer making out on his sofa, watching *Survivorman,* versing each other on Guitar Hero, and, well, making out on his sofa.

Except I can't help but wonder if his preference to be at his house is more of a desire to avoid mine. Not that I blame him. At my house he'd risk facing my protective father, grandfather, and three uncles. But if Trevor's going to stick around, he should get to know them, right?

We finally reach the exit of the lot with the blessing of the green traffic light. Trevor makes a sharp right, and once he's in gear, takes his hand off the stick shift for a moment and caresses my kneecap with his thumb.

"You want to stop for a snow cone?" he asks.

"That sounds great."

"Cool. After, we'll head over to my place."

I don't argue because even though I'd rather go to my house, I don't want to make Trevor do anything he doesn't want to do.

I only hope he feels the same way about me.

We're on his couch. Our lips lock, hot and heavy. Hundreds of waterfalls begin to cascade through my blood. My hands rest on his belt loops, just as immobile as they are with the clay. But Trevor doesn't seem to mind.

Then he starts to run his hand up the back of my shirt.

The waterfalls I felt earlier turn into glaciers. Although it feels sort of nice, I'm scared.

Next he starts to kiss my neck. I want to stop, but there's a piece of me that wants to keep going because my body feels light as air.

It's exciting one moment. And terrifying the next. Actually, it's like being tickled and pinched at the same time. But mostly tickled.

Trevor's long legs shift on the couch. I wiggle over to the side to give him more room, but when he rolls on top of me, my head sinks into the smooshy sofa cushion.

I'm not sure where to put my arms so I wrap them around his neck. His elbows jut out like pelican wings.

Trevor wiggles his neck loose, allowing me to look into his dark brown eyes. I reach up and finger the thin circle of his earring, his earlobe soft as peach fuzz. I laugh as I begin to trace his mouth. "Your lips are so blue." Remnants of the snow cone.

"And yours are ruby red." He kisses me again. "Let's go somewhere more comfortable."

I stare over at the clock on the DVR. I've got an hour before I should leave for the Banshee.

"Okay," I say, in keeping with the "easygoing" personality that Trevor seems to adore about me. And it is okay. There's no need for me to panic because I haven't said yes to anything other than getting more comfortable.

He smiles widely as he heaves me up from the couch and we walk down the hallway, which is decorated with stark black-and-white landmark photos from the cosmopolitan cities his parents jet to: the Eiffel Tower. Big Ben. The Empire State Building.

We whisk into his room, where the afternoon light filters in through the window blinds. He tows me onto his bed. We tumble over each other, giggle, and stretch out our legs.

"Molly?" His lips touch my ear as he says it; goose bumps perk along my arm.

"Uh-huh?"

"I love you," he whispers.

Love? He *loves* me? My heart thumps inside my chest. He pulls back so I can touch his face, smooth yet whiskery in some spots. "I love you, too, Trevor."

He leans down again, nuzzles his face into my hair, kisses me on the cheek, then my forehead, and the tip of my nose. This feels so good. This is love! We only whispered it, but we said it. Love.

He gets up from the bed.

I wouldn't mind having him back here with me where my blood still feels pumpy and strong, but I'm grateful that he respects me enough—loves me enough—to stop us from going any further today.

I sit up on my elbows to find Trevor closing his bedroom door. "What are you doing?" I ask.

"Locking the door. Just in case."

Now I'm freezing all over like a blue snow cone.

Jesus, Mary, and Joseph. Aren't we rushing things?

"Trevor?"

He dives back on the bed and wraps his arms around me. "We have time. Don't worry."

"No." I gently twist out of his arms. "It's not that."

"Then what?" I'm not sure if he looks concerned or annoyed.

"This is too . . . *much*." I bite my lower lip.

Trevor just stares at me. "Uh . . . okay."

My mouth goes dry. I sit up all the way and pull my knees to my chest. "We've only been together three months."

He creeps closer. "Look, we care about each other."

"I just don't feel like I'm ready."

"Well, how will you know unless you try?" His fingers brush against my cheek. The dimple's in full bloom.

"Trevor."

He leans over and kisses me, his hands buried once again in my hair.

Other girls would kill to be with him. How can I even question this?

He's kissing my neck again, but I'm thinking about Felicia. How they did God-knows-what in this bedroom and now they're not together anymore. As he begins to kiss my collarbone, I pull away.

Trevor groans and falls back down on the bed, rubbing his eyes with his fists.

I lean over him, a rope of my hair dangling over his chest. "I'm sorry."

He sighs.

I was hoping for "It's okay, Molly, let's slow things down." But he doesn't say anything, which further proves my newfound theory that if I want to keep him, I'm going to have to rise to the occasion, but this is all happening too fast.

"Give me a minute?" Before Trevor can answer, I get up from his bed and step across the cool-to-the-touch Pergo floor beneath my feet. Daddy and the uncles hate fake wood. "Crap-o" is what they call it.

I shut the door to his bathroom behind me and stop in front of the white-framed mirror hanging over the sink, then contemplate doing a he-loves-me, he-loves-me-not routine with my freckles, but turn on the water instead, so it sounds like I'm doing something important in here.

About a month ago, Aunt Tipper and I stacked pint

glasses behind the bar at the Banshee, while the final few minutes of a soccer game aired on the monitors above us. Despite the audio calamity in the bar, Aunt Tip offered an out-of-the-blue confession doused in her strong Irish accent. "I had my heart broken when I was your age."

I eyed her gray hair, which spirals atop her head like a metallic cinnamon roll. She said, "I'm seventy-one, yet I can still describe the sour feeling in my stomach after Finnegan Walsh broke it off with me, because a few days later, the bastard was already with another girl."

She pursed her lips and clutched a pint glass, clearly having a vivid recollection of the whole event, which was, like, more than fifty years ago. "Molly, no one tells you that when you fall in love, you lose your perspective."

She must have read my confusion. "I'm saying, don't rush it with that boyfriend of yours, girl. The faster you move, the more you'll have to regret if things don't work out."

I don't want regrets. If Trevor really loves me, he'll be patient, I have to believe that. I turn off the streaming faucet and take a deep breath.

Back in his room, Trevor lounges on his bed, his ankles crossed and arms comfortably tucked behind his head.

I sit on the corner of the mattress. Trevor comes up from behind and wraps his arms around me.

I take hold of one of his hands, then turn and kiss

him on the cheek. It's less than what he wants, I know, but I hope he doesn't mind. "It's getting late, Trevor."

He lets out a big fire-breathing breath.

Yep, he minds.

"Fine, let's go." He vaults off the bed, unlocks the door, flings it open, and disappears into the hallway.

I stand up and stop short of the doorway of Trevor's room, where in a glass tank, Trevor's black-spotted leopard gecko, Vinny, stares at me from atop reptile carpet. He licks an eyeball with his tongue.

"He's mad at me now, Vinny. What am I going to do?"

But he doesn't have any answers for me. Figures.

A few moments later, Trevor drives me over to the Banshee. The houses outside flicker past like a fast-tempo slideshow. Palm trees line the sidewalks but are so still in the muggy, inert air they look like scarecrows. The Killers crank through the speakers, relieving Trevor of having to say anything to me. He won't look at me, either. Or put his hand on my knee like he did earlier.

Fifteen minutes ago, he couldn't keep his hands off me. And, like, twenty-five minutes ago, he told me he loved me! This can only be a flash-forward into what will happen if I want to move along at a snail's pace: he's gonna check out. Leave. Suddenly our relation-ship now feels like a time bomb, tick-tick-tocking.

We reach downtown Hilldale. Trevor pulls up to the curb a few storefronts down from the Banshee's black-shingled exterior, sandwiched between a smoke shop and a quilting store. Two pale green stained-glass windows conceal the inside of the pub from passersby. Trevor doesn't even turn off the engine.

"Thanks for the ride," I shout over the music, with perhaps too much lilt in my voice. He keeps his gaze focused ahead at the white parallel lines of the crosswalk. "Trevor?"

"You're welcome."

"Trevor." I reach over and turn off the stereo. His jaw is so tight right now I can see the muscles twitch. My hand rests on his thigh. "So, I'll see you in the morning?"

He shakes his head. "I have conditioning at the gym." He doesn't twist toward me or look me in the eye.

I can't have him pulling away. "Trevor?" I angle myself closer to him; the firm slope of his chin juts out like a cliff. "I'll make it worth the wait."

What did I just say?!

He shakes his head. "Don't say it if you don't mean it, Molly."

"No, I really mean it." It's so easy to say when I know I'm going to lose him if I don't.

"Okay, then," he says, his voice noticeably softening. "I'm not trying to be a jerk. I just . . . want to get closer to you."

"I feel the same way. I freaked out, that's all."

He doesn't answer, but his scowl is gone. Maybe that signals a truce.

"So," I say, "are we still gonna hang out tomorrow night?" I'm literally crossing my fingers behind my back in hopes that he's not going to break up with me at this moment.

"Sure," he says. Still, he's not swooping in for a kiss.

I reach for my messenger bag from the backseat of his car, lifting it carefully to protect the mask Trevor gave me, which is inside. I hop down from the Jeep, shut the door behind me, and wave more cheerfully than I feel while Trevor drives away.

I wish that Vinny the gecko had spoken up a few minutes ago when I asked him what I should do. But Daddy always says all the answers we'll ever need lie within. Even so, I haven't a clue as to where to start looking.

THE BANSHEE'S WAKE
WEEKLY SCHEDULE
(Always Subject to Change)

MONDAY: IRISH CEILI DANCING WITH AGNES FLYNN
TUESDAY: ALL-YOU-CAN-EAT SHEPHERD'S PIE
WEDNESDAY: IRISH FOLK MUSIC NIGHT
(LIVE OR JUKEBOX)
THURSDAY: TGIAF (THANK GOD IT'S ALMOST FRIDAY)
$3 PINTS
FRIDAY: BANGERS, BEANS, AND BATTLE OF THE BANDS
SATURDAY: KARAOKE WITH HOOTS
SUNDAY: OPEN-MIKE NIGHT
WITH CLEM THE FLYING SCOTSMAN

Face to face with the heavy black door of the Banshee, I yank the dull brass handle and walk inside. My eyes take a moment to adjust to the dimly lit, narrow, red-walled corridor adorned with posters of Ireland—castles, green hills, and rocky coastlines.

Above me on the ceiling droops a tattered green, white, and orange Irish flag. Framed glossy pictures that chronicle random nights at the pub scatter along the wall: happy pink faces—youthful and old—that represent the quintessential stereotype of the carousing Irish.

There's the picture of Mom and Daddy holding me when I was only a few months old, bundled in blankets as if the Southern California weather in Hilldale would somehow freeze my skin.

I gaze up at my favorite picture, the one of my beautiful, dark-haired mother next to Daddy on their wedding day in front of the Church of St. Anne Shandon in Cork, Ireland. Mom's family scraped together all they had so she could be married in her childhood parish wearing a gown made of Irish lace and hearing the clock tower bells of the Shandon chiming through all of Cork.

Daddy always says he couldn't believe that a good Catholic girl like Mom even considered being with a ruffian like him. He dropped out of school at fourteen because he spent more time in the headmaster's office than the actual classroom, so he turned to woodworking at the elbow of Granddad. Mom met him years later when he was called in to repair a wooden beam on the ferry that her dad owned and operated across the River Lee.

Daddy would soon return to her bearing the gift of a whittled wooden sculpture of her—an offering that captured her heart and now resides on the nightstand in my bedroom. It's one of a few things I have left of her since she died of pancreatic cancer when I was four. It doesn't matter that I've lived most of my life without her. I still miss her, in the same way I want the warmth of a blanket when I'm cold, except nothing—not even my loving father or my caring family—can warm the empty part of me that yearns for her.

I move toward the end of the hallway and pass the shadowboxed autographed album cover of Van Morrison's *Astral Weeks*. It's Aunt Tip's most prized possession. She met the man, kissed the man, and had the guts to quote him to his face, "It's a fantabulous night to make romance!"

Aunt Tip is Granddad's younger sister and the first of the family to move to America, about twenty-five years ago, after she married Clem, who was at the time a wealthy Scotsman and small-time entrepreneur of barrel-shaped cheese. Now he's co-owner of their only living offspring in old town Hilldale, the Banshee's Wake.

I can hear the loud mumble of voices inside the pub and I hesitate, stopping short of the doorway. I try to shake Trevor off and lift my sagging shoulders—posture! posture!—then step over the threshold into the pub.

"There she is!" Shout-outs whirl around me.

"There's our girl!"

"Molly!"

I wave back to some of the gray and balding clientele and inhale the delicious smell of rosemary and thyme wafting from the Banshee's famous cauldron of beef stew simmering in the kitchen.

The lively fiddle-heavy rendition of "Cotton-Eyed Joe" performed by the Chieftains pipes over the speakers.

"Afternoon, Molly Brigid!" Aunt Tipper waves from behind the well-worn rectangular oak bar in the middle of the restaurant. Her long gray hair coils atop her head in her signature bun.

"Hey, Aunt Tip."

"You okay there, love?"

Crap. Even in the frame of dark wood-paneled walls and weak light, I can't hide my stupid face, apparently still flushed from my afternoon with Trevor. "I'm fine. Long day is all." A flashback of Trevor kissing my neck sends a quiver through my body.

"Hey, Mol!" Over in the corner, Granddad, Daddy, and the uncles sit around a table, waving me over. "Come on over here, Molly girl!" Daddy calls.

Aunt Tip warns, "You'd better go to them before they make too much of a ruckus."

I look past mirror-etched ale logos, past red vinyl booths where a few families contemplate the menus. At one table, a little freckle-faced boy bites into the Banshee's warm PB and J. Gooey peanut butter oozes onto his plate. I wave and he offers a peanut butter smile, which makes me laugh until I refocus my attention and move toward my Irish men.

"What's taking you so long, Molly B?" Uncle Murph yells.

Uncle Garrett adds, "That's right, girl! Speed it up!" Daddy, Granddad, and my uncles left Ireland almost two decades ago, yet their country remains captured in their vocal cords like gruff air trapped inside the belly of a bagpipe.

It wasn't until after Grandma Maeve died of an eight-year battle with Hodgkin's disease that Granddad took Aunt Tip's offer to join her and Clem in Southern California. At the time, Mom and Daddy had been married almost a year and were living with Mom's overbearing family. Daddy said that I was growing inside her when they made the decision to follow Granddad and the uncles to California.

Once Daddy and the family arrived in America, they rented our house in South Hilldale, and although Granddad would never pound another hammer in his life, his sons picked up where he left off as a woodworker in Cork and established themselves as craftsmen—four handsome lads who could lay a wooden floor that would never fail beneath your feet. "A lifetime warranty is our guarantee." That's the O'Keefe Brothers promise.

That phrase always rattles my brain. If only my mother had come with a lifetime guarantee.

Once I reach the table, I lean toward the birthday boy first, his jowls bobbing against my cheek. "Well, there she is!"

"Happy birthday, Granddad!" I pull back and tousle his wooly web of white hair. "You don't look a day over seventy," I say.

Granddad grins and softly pinches my chin. "Glad you're here, love."

"And look at the rest of you." I wave over the circle of Daddy and my three uncles, who wear neckties and suit jackets, definitely not their usual couture. "Wow. Am I even at the right table? I hardly recognize you without your work boots and grimy jeans."

"Stop being a smarty-arse and come give your pop a hug," Daddy says, his cloudless-blue-sky eyes sparkling below the thick auburn hair that has receded in recent years.

"If you insist." I bend into his open arms and smell the cool pine of his aftershave.

"And where've you been? With *that boy*?"

"He has a name, Daddy."

"Yeah, *Rude*."

I roll my eyes.

"Your da's right," says Uncle Garrett, his mouth full of dinner roll and a line of butter trickling down his chin. "Ain't no respectful boy would drop you off like you were a fish being tossed in a bucket." He swallows a generous gulp of Guinness, causing a dark curl from his head to boing.

"Ha!" chortles Uncle Murph, whose arms I go to

next. I rub the luster of his smooth, bald head. "Hey, Mol. Look at Casanova over there." As he laughs, his large belly threatens to pop the buttons on his shirt. "Garrett, you can't feckin' manage to chew your food before swallowing, let alone treat a lady right."

"Well"—Uncle Garrett wipes his mouth with his sleeve, completely missing the butter on his chin—"at least I *got* myself a love life."

"Oh!" Uncle Murph flutters his hands in the air. "Is that what you call it? Going from girl to girl on any given night." Uncle Garrett's handsome, chiseled features make him a woman magnet. "A lady deserves respect. Ain't that right, Mol?"

"I'm staying out of this one," I say, and move over to Uncle Rourke, who points his bulbous soupspoon at me. "Smart girl, you are." His feathery light-brown hair wisps over his John Lennon–style wire-rimmed glasses. He gives me a hug before he looks down to poke the melted lid of cheese covering his bowl of onion soup.

Daddy motions me over to him. I sit and rest my messenger bag at my feet. "You want a cheese and pickle sandwich?"

My stomach is still uneasy from Trevor. "I'm good, actually."

"Well, that's a first," says Granddad, surprised. "Never heard you turn down the ol' cheese and pickle."

"Something wrong?" Daddy's eyes become microscopes.

I smile to deflect any concern. "No, I'm fine. I just

ate before I got here." It's important to me that Daddy likes Trevor, so I exaggerate. "Trevor made us sandwiches after we did some homework." Which reminds me I've got a precalc test tomorrow. Must study.

"He a nice boy, Molly?" asks Granddad.

"I've got my doubts," Daddy says, sawing into what's left of his thick steak with a serrated knife.

"Daddy, you don't even *know* him." Trevor's the first guy I've dated, even though, unbeknownst to my family, I've been with a few different guys in my life. Nothing compared to Vanessa's track record.

"I do know one thing, Molly," Daddy says with a pink chunk of medium-rare meat poked through his fork. "That boy should have the courtesy to walk up to the door and knock when he picks you up instead of him blasting that horn of his."

"Your pop's right, Molly," says Uncle Murph. "You got to show the boy that he must *earn* your respect."

"You guys are so old-fashioned," I say, trying to blow it off.

"Bah! Old-fashioned!" Uncle Garrett says.

Uncle Rourke shakes his head. "It's about common courtesy. We just want to make sure you're watching out for yourself, is all. That you're setting the bar high."

"Over his head, that's for sure!" Granddad agrees.

"Could all of you give me and Mol a moment alone?" Daddy must sense my discomfort.

"Sure thing, Owen," says Uncle Rourke.

Granddad pulls his bib from his neck. "We got to

get going on that stage anyway, right, boys?" They slide out of the booth, Uncle Garrett giving me a wink and mouthing *good luck*.

"I tell you what, Molly." Daddy pinches the edge of his napkin and dabs the corners of his mouth. "Next time you go out with that boy, he's coming inside the house and I'm gonna have a chat with him."

"Oh, no you won't." I'm walking on eggshells with Trevor as it is now.

"Oh, yes I will," says Daddy.

"C'mon," I plead.

"It's that or you won't be getting in that car of his with him." He rubs the knob of his nose.

"Daddy."

"I'm your da and I deserve to know who this boy is. You got lots of freedom, girl. I trust you, you know that. But this is my right, Molly. You're my gold, girl. I want to know for myself whether I can trust this boy. You got to give me that, will ya?"

I sigh. This does not bode well for me or Trevor. "He's scared of you, Daddy."

"Good." Daddy nods. "When you gonna see him again?"

"I'm not sure," I lie.

"You're not sure, are you?" He's on to me.

"We might go out tomorrow night, but it's not definite."

"Well, whenever it is, he's coming inside if he expects you to get in that car with him, you hear?"

Crap-poop-hell! There's no point arguing because

the more defensive I get, the more worried he'll be. Play it cool.

"Fine." I jump up from my seat and grab my school bag, eager to escape. "I'm gonna go get Buttons."

"Good idea." He glances over to the small stage, where Granddad and the uncles bustle to organize themselves. "Looks like the others are almost ready for us." He reaches out for my hand, gives it a squeeze. "You know I'm not trying to be a big bully. It's 'cause I love you, Molly."

"I know. Love you, too." I peck his forehead and walk to the back of the restaurant, down a small hallway; inside the quiet haven of Aunt Tip's dark, wood-paneled office, I fall back on the scratchy couch. I want to call Trevor and ask him point-blank if he's going to dump me. If he is, I can spare myself the humiliation of telling him he's got to have a chat with my dad. But I don't think I could handle the truth right now.

"Molly?" Aunt Tip calls from behind the door. "Grab your squeeze box. The boys are ready to fire it up."

"Coming!" I get up from the couch. Buttons, my accordion, sits beside Aunt Tip's desk. Daddy said Mom never really learned how to play. Maybe it was her own rebellion against her father, who expected her to learn. Mom was more of a singer than a musician, but of the few things she brought with her from Ireland, the accordion was one of them. Daddy gave it to me when I was six, and I named it Buttons the moment I touched it.

I lift Buttons out of his case. Closed, he's about the size of a shoebox, but when I undo the clasps and let him hum out for his first yawn, he expands with the grace of a fan. The fingers on my right hand stretch over the twenty-one black treble buttons while my left hand twiddles over the eight on the other side.

It may have taken me all day, but finally I feel at ease. If only the rest of my life could play out as easily as a tune from Buttons.

After school on Friday, Vanessa holds her French fry in midair. She sits on top of the tiki tower at the mall's Aloha Burger playground. "So wait, you told Trevor Schultz to slow down?" Her head of long brown hair jostles. "Ha! Must have been the first time he'd heard that!"

She pops the fry in her mouth and stomps her feet, startling the screaming kids in the fake volcano pit below. Vanessa is not Trevor's biggest fan. She agrees that he's beautiful, but she thinks he's full of himself. Plus, she hates his ex, Felicia, who gave Nessa a few years of hell for having been held back in third grade.

I grab hold of the totem pole that leads to the slide. "Ness, he was just frustrated is all. He was fine at school today."

"You sure?" She squints her brown eyes at me. "Mol, you guys just waved good-bye to each other in the parking lot after school. There was none of that slobbery buh-bye kissing I saw at the beginning of the week."

She's right, I didn't get my after-school kiss. Maybe I'm fooling myself, but I try to be casual about this. "Well, we're still on for tonight."

She stands, extending to her long, leggy height, and surveys the slide below her. "So, are you going to surrender to his charms, or not?"

"I don't want to lose him, but Ness, I don't know if I'm ready for the next step."

She plops down on the top of the slide. "That's a tough one. But truthfully, Mol, it's like what I said the other day: he's expecting to pass go and collect his two hundred dollars. The boy wants to advance."

"Yeah, but we haven't been together for that long. I mean, three months? It's not that long, is it? I don't think I even made eye contact with Trevor for, like, three *years*."

Vanessa laughs. "Well, not all of us are as freakish as you." With that, she curves down the corkscrew of the lava slide with her bronzed arms raised toward the sky. "Yee-haw!" she screams when she reaches the bottom and falls into the pit of plastic balls.

I applaud gleefully in return.

"C'mon, Mol! I gotta pee, then we can get our bootylicious Halloween costumes."

Two moms scowl at her as they help their little boys totter around the fake fire pit.

"Bootylicious?" I whisper to myself, knowing that my own flat booty is not so *licious,* whatever that means. "I'll meet you outside the restroom," I say.

Vanessa waves and bounds off toward the ladies' room.

Nessa and I met in elementary school after she had to repeat the third grade. I was definitely on the dorkish side of the social spectrum but Nessa saw that I was somewhat shy and needed help surviving the dog-eat-dog world of the public education system. I welcomed her bossy, brassy confidence with open arms.

By seventh grade, as we muddled through the world of junior high, Vanessa started bringing her mom's *Cosmopolitan* magazines to school. We'd sit behind the gym during lunch, flip through them, and take those quizzes inside. At first, our comparative magazine quiz scores couldn't be more opposite: Me, Style Disaster; Vanessa, Fashion Catwalker.

Nessa urged me to wear my hair down and gave me the nerve to ask Daddy for contact lenses. I did, but only after I broke my only pair of glasses while performing the Who's "Pinball Wizard" with Uncle Rourke onstage at the Banshee, when they flew off and I accidentally stomped on the frames in my search for them. At the end of eighth grade when I got my braces off, Nessa claimed I went from Invisible Wallflower to Double-Take Chick. Still, when I see myself in the mirror, I can't get beyond the vision of the ordinary, freckled, round-cheeked reflection that is me.

I wait for Nessa outside the bathroom until she

emerges, fastening the belt on her extra-low-rise jeans. "All set!"

We walk toward a store called Flashback in the outdoor mall, but Vanessa comes to an abrupt halt in front of a window display of Lady Chatterley's Lingerie: mannequins wearing fuzzy, tiger-striped baby dolls and solid orange and black panty-bra combos. "Ooh," says Vanessa, "lookie there."

The slightly parted lips of the mannequins give one the impression that merely wearing these undergarments is a passion-rendering experience. "Can you even imagine us walking into Zach Hegel's Halloween party wearing those?" She laughs and curls her fingers in the air like claws. "Meow!"

"I'm not wearing that, kitty cat."

Nessa snarls. *"Fft! Fft!"* Her arms drop to her sides. "Wait, does that mean you're not going with me?"

I wince a little. I haven't run any plans by Trevor yet, so I don't want to obligate myself. "Trevor might come along, if that's okay."

"Of course." She rolls her eyes. "I wouldn't want you to die of separation anxiety, but it'd be cool if you could hang with your old pal Vanessa once in a while. I guess I'll take the package deal if that's my only choice."

I'd rather go alone with him, but I don't want to upset Vanessa since I've already spent so much time away from her these last three months, which have not been as carefree as others for her and me.

Vanessa's attention zooms back to the window display. "We should at least consider buying some of those." She points to the fuzzy black boas around the necks of the mannequins, which make them look like they're being choked by feather dusters.

"I've got a forty-dollar budget here, Ness."

"Let's see how much they cost."

At the front of the store, tiered tables display panties and bras, all arranged according to color, a rainbow swirl of underwear.

"Ha! Look at these!" Vanessa croons, holding up a pair of pink velvet panties with fluffy pom-poms at the side. She places them on her head. "They're panties *and* earmuffs!"

I laugh. She can be such a cheeseball; truthfully, this is the part of her I love the best. She twirls the same style in yellow around her finger. "Here, Mol, try them on!"

Nessa crowns me with the pom-pom undies and I laugh once again, this time with an unfeminine snort.

"Nice hats." A familiar, superior-sounding voice interrupts our fun.

We turn and see Felicia Mitchell, as in, Trevor's ex-girlfriend. She's at a display of skimpy Lycra three-for-twenty-dollars bikinis a few tables away from us.

Rocks pile up in my stomach. I react to Felicia the same way I react to bees: I tend to run in the opposite direction when I see either. And, as is true with bees, I never approach Felicia willingly for fear of being stung.

"Hey, it's Little Miss Sunshine," Nessa says under her breath.

Felicia flicks her long, straight hair behind her

shoulders. Her wedge-heel sandals add inches to her already tall frame, and her strappy gray dress clings to her body like it's been applied with a paint roller. She glowers at Nessa, then at me.

I grab hold of the pom-pom near my ear, slide the skivvies off my head, and smooth my hair. Nessa doesn't budge.

Felicia eyeballs the yellow panties crumpled in my hand. "That's not his favorite color," she says with a sneer.

Nessa clears her throat and waits for me to say something, but instead I shrink to the size of a Polly Pocket, because Felicia's right, I don't know Trevor's favorite color. In fact, she knows nine months more about Trevor than I do. With her standing a few feet away, I have to wonder why Trevor would choose a less qualified yet easygoing me over an experienced beauty-pageant queen like Felicia.

Nessa approaches Felicia and nudges up close while I continue to amass droplets of sweat on my upper lip. "I think it's important that you shut your pie hole, Felicia. That is, unless you're really trying to be as vile as you seem, to which I say, bravo on your performance." Nessa applauds. The girl can dole out a comeback at the right moment, unlike me, who never thinks of a response until hours later, when it's too late.

Unscathed, Felicia sidesteps Nessa and aims her stinger directly at me. "I'm just being honest. Really, I'm surprised that you and Trevor have lasted this long." She shrugs matter-of-factly and slinks away, leaving us to look at her perfectly defined butt.

"Mol, you can't let her talk to you like that," Vanessa grumbles. "*Say* something to her."

But it's too late. Felicia's out the door.

I dip my hands down into the mound of panties below, my lower lip trembling. "She's right. He's tired of me. I can feel it."

Vanessa puts her hand on my shoulder. "Look, if that's true, then it's his loss and we'll have empirical evidence that he sucks, just like I always thought he did," she says with a wink.

I chuckle in spite of myself. "Can't you *pretend* to be sensitive to my situation?"

"Fine, I will *pretend* to be sensitive, but don't think for a minute that if he dumps you it's *your* loss." Nessa grabs my hand and leads us out of Lady Chatterley's. "Let's forget about the boas. What do you think about bright neon spandex?"

I stare at her, amazed. "What kind of costume is that?"

"I don't know, but I can guarantee that no one at the party will be able to take their eyes off us." Nessa ruffles my hair.

As she tows me toward Flashback, I can't shake the distance I felt from Trevor today and Felicia's in-your-face nearness, both of which hold me at gunpoint. The fear that I'm going to lose Trevor is at close range, but I know it's a bullet I'm not ready to bite.

I never fuss about clothes, but tonight is different. Flung across every surface of my room—my double bed, my desk chair, my music stand—is the carnage of clothes cast aside. If I think too much about something— like what I should wear on my date with Trevor—I seize up, like now. Trevor will be here any minute, and I'm still in my bra and underwear.

I had hoped Daddy would forget his plan to "chat" with Trevor and head directly over to the Banshee after work. But he and the uncles came home a half hour ago, and they continue to mill around downstairs, the echo of their voices bouncing off the wall-to-wall hardwood floors.

It's at moments like this, though, when I'm thankful to have my own separate space where I can panic in private. Daddy and the uncles converted the attic into my bedroom when I was eleven. It took them two years to finish since it was a part-time endeavor, plus they had to lay pipe for my own bathroom. It worked out well for everyone, though. Daddy didn't have to share a room with Uncle Rourke anymore and I got more privacy. When I turned thirteen, I cried uncontrollably for no reason, and it was nice to have the luxury of hiding it away from everyone else in the house.

Trevor is going to be here soon! Urgh. My stomach swells. The bottle of Pepto-Bismol I drank from twenty minutes earlier offered only temporary relief; the woozy feeling floods back, so I run to the bathroom and take another swig, coughing when the chalky aftertaste hits.

I stumble back into my bedroom and plop down on my bed, where the whittled statue of Mom sits on my nightstand. The mask Trevor made me sits on my desk. I wonder if Mom and I would have had the kind of relationship where I could talk openly with her about Trevor and how to handle all these feelings inside.

I grab the wooden statue, rub the smooth curve of her neck. The last time I was with my mother I was four years old in Saint Didacus Church, a few blocks away. Mom's boxy urn rested on a table beneath the impossibly high ceilings of its stained-glass chapel. Daddy said that Mom was so adamant about being cremated that a month before she died, she contacted the priest at St. Didacus herself to make sure they'd allow for a cremation memorial. "She always said that when she died, she wanted to be scattered somewhere, not stuck inside a casket."

Still, it's the image of the urn—the small maple-wood box—that I remember most about the day of her memorial. I knew she was inside it, and it scared me to think about how someone managed to squeeze her whole soft self into it. From that day on, Daddy, Grand-dad, the uncles, and Aunt Tipper couldn't get me to set foot inside Saint Didacus.

I don't believe in monsters under my bed anymore, but I do believe there's something in that church that will swallow me whole if I enter. Every year Daddy goes to Mass on the anniversary of Mom's death in July, and every year he asks me to come along. Every year, I refuse.

A horn honks. Trevor!

I set Mom back on the nightstand, roll off my bed, pluck the drooping short denim skirt from my lamp-shade, and wriggle it over my hips. I reach for my pink T-shirt puddled on the floor, slip into my flip-flops, and shove the bottle of Pepto-Bismol from my bathroom into my canvas shoulder bag.

I clamber down the stairs and past the empty bed-rooms of Daddy and Uncle Rourke. They're still down-stairs, but I might be able to get to the door first.

When I jump down the last few steps into the entry hall, Daddy has already beaten me to the door. His hand grips the doorknob.

"Please don't do this, Daddy," I beg.

He holds up a calloused hand. "We talked about this, Mol. It's this, or you don't go." Resistance is futile.

"Be nice. Please, Daddy. I really like him."

"I don't bite." Urgh. That's not exactly reassuring,

because he straightens up, adding another two inches to his six-foot-four frame, opens the front door, and waves Trevor inside.

I stand behind Daddy, who looms like a giant in his steel-toed boots, and watch Trevor hesitate, then slowly climb out of his Jeep and walk up the cement path in slow motion, his face pale and puzzled.

I dread Trevor's first sight of the shrine to our Catholic roots in our entry hall, decor my mother left behind and no one dared to remove. I cast a glance at the portrait of the Virgin Mother beneath her layers of robes. I don't know how to contact her, but it doesn't stop me from offering my plea: "Please help me," I whisper.

"Hello, boy," Daddy says. From behind him I mouth *Sorry*.

Trevor stops short of the porch step and slips a hand into his deep-pocketed shorts.

"Um, hi." Trevor is normally so confident, but now he is suddenly shy.

"So, then. I'm Molly's father. Owen." Daddy extends a huge paw toward Trevor, and Trevor reluctantly offers his own. Daddy grips it hard and Trevor squeezes back.

"Daddy, this is Trevor." I tap him on the shoulder and he finally lets Trevor have his hand back.

"Please." Daddy waves him inside. "Come in." We follow Daddy down the hallway behind his ogrelike stomping, past the oval family portrait of the men and me with our instruments on our laps, and past my own saint, Saint Brigid, who, for some reason, holds a bowl of fire.

Trevor shoots me a *What the hell?* expression. I shrug in helplessness.

Daddy clomps into the den, where the uncles stand up from their horseshoe of La-Z-Boy chairs facing the big-screen TV. The uncles look barbaric with their stained work shirts and glue-streaked boots. Trevor's shoulders slump, so I ease up to him, place my hand on his elbow for comfort.

"Hello there!" says Uncle Garrett in a friendly tone.

"Yes, good to see you," adds Uncle Rourke, always a gentleman. "Glad you came inside."

This isn't so bad. They're friendly men, Trevor has to notice that.

Uncle Murph steps in closer to us. "So, then." He rubs his bald head with the flat of his palm and asks Trevor sternly, "Tell me, boy, what *are* you if you ain't Irish?" This is Uncle Murph's favorite joke.

"Excuse me?" Trevor cocks his head.

"It's a joke, Trevor," I say, attempting to sound encouraging.

"Oh." He nods, still tense.

"That's right, a joke. Kind of." Uncle Murph takes a quick swig of his beer. "So then, again. What *are* you if you ain't Irish?"

Trevor shrugs.

"Ashamed!" Uncle Murph slaps Trevor on the back, his laugh deep and wheezy, like he's just spent the day in a coal mine. Trevor musters a crooked smile.

"It never gets old for ya, does it, Murph?" asks Uncle Garrett, back to reclining on his La-Z-Boy.

"No," he answers, shaking his head, "it don't."

Daddy pats my shoulder. "Molly? Give us a moment."

Hell-damn-argh! All of them? That's not fair. Trevor looks at me with the shivery appearance of a wet dog.

I give his hand a reassuring squeeze and say to Daddy, "The movie starts soon, so can you, you know, be quick?" Trevor offers me a tight smile. There is no movie.

Daddy nods. "Go on, Molly. We're just gonna have a quick chat."

At this, Uncle Garrett crunches the footrest in with his calves, and all of them sit up straight in their chairs, like they're knights of the round coffee table. They might as well be pointing swords at poor Trevor, whose eyes fix on me for assurance that he'll live. I send him another apologetic smile and walk out of the den backward as Daddy looms over Trevor and waves him to sit on the squat coffee table smack in the middle of the La-Z-Boys.

I press my ear against the wall in the entry hall, but only muffled voices waft through.

A quick knock on the front door jolts me, and I rush to open it. Our neighbor, Dede Fenway, squeals, "Oh, thank heavens you're here!"

She storms into the house, wringing her French-manicured hands. Dede isn't a theatrical woman, so I'm concerned about the panicked expression on her pretty thirtysomething face.

"Is everything okay?" I ask.

Dede swallows hard. "I'm so sorry to bother you,

Molly, but I just got a call from my mother. She tripped over the ottoman in her living room and fell."

I gasp. Dede's mom is elderly and quite fragile. No wonder Dede is so frantic. "Is she all right?"

"I'm not sure. She may have broken something." Dede's voice quavers. "Would you mind babysitting Claire tonight? Robert and I don't want to schlep her to the emergency room. Who knows how long we'll be there?"

Before I can even begin to worm out of this, Dede pulls me in for a big hug.

"Oh, thank you, Molly," she gushes. "Thank you!"

Wait a minute, here. I didn't say yes!

Dede releases me from her clutches and stares at me with watery eyes, which render me completely helpless. As much as I want to keep this date with Trevor, I do feel bad for her. She has been dealing with her mother's poor health for the past few months. My mind tells my heart that Trevor will understand, but given our recent history, my heart doesn't really believe it.

"Lemme just tell my dad and I'll be right over," I say.

"Molly, you're a lifesaver," Dede says through a sniffle. "I'll see you in a few minutes!"

She flies out the door, buzzing with nervous energy. I peer out the window and watch as she jogs across our yard and into her own.

I wish I could've just gone with her and disappeared instead of having to face the Irish Inquisition and a ticked-off Trevor.

In the den, all eyes turn to me. Daddy's finger stays pointed at Trevor, who sits on his hands, surrounded by the men of my house, who are tilting forward on their La-Z-Boys like guard dogs ready to pounce. "Excuse me, Daddy?"

"Give us another minute, eh?"

"Dede stopped by. She needs to take her mom to the hospital. I'm going to watch Claire while she's gone." I look at Trevor now. "Which means I can't go out tonight."

Trevor stands up and rushes to me, as if I might be lying to get him out of this. "Cool. Then I'll just call you later." He turns to look back at Daddy, Granddad, and the uncles. "It was nice meeting you." He says it with more relief than sincerity.

Daddy stands. "We'll see you next time, lad."

Trevor doesn't bother to kiss me or linger with a longer good-bye. He bolts. I shake my head at the La-Z-Boy brigade and run through the hall and out the front door after Trevor.

"Hey, wait up!" I shout as Trevor gets into his Jeep.

"Man, what was *that* about? It was like facing a firing squad!"

I stand in the street, outside the driver's-side door. "Trevor, I'm so sorry. They're a little protective."

"Uh, yeah. That's pretty obvious."

"They didn't, like, threaten you or something, did they?"

Trevor lets out a sarcastic laugh. "Let's see, your dad wants me to knock at the door when I come pick you up. And the bald one asked me what my intentions were—"

"That's Uncle Murph."

"Whatever. The one with the glasses—"

"Uncle Rourke."

"Yeah, well." Trevor waves his hand, like it shouldn't matter who's who. "He said something about patience conquering destiny."

"It's an Irish proverb—" I start to explain.

"I get it, Molly, but I don't need to be lectured by your family."

Looks like my heart was right. Trevor doesn't seem to understand. "We're close, is all. They want to make sure I'm safe."

"Well, all I know is that my parents trust me."

"What?" Does he think my dad and uncles don't trust me? "They just want to know who you are, Trevor. We've been going out for three months. I've held them off as long as possible. It was time for them to meet you, don't you think?"

He throws his hands up. "It's them against me."

"No, it's not like that," I say.

"Look, it doesn't matter. Just go babysit. I'll call you tomorrow or something."

Or *something*?

All of a sudden, it's difficult to breathe. The minute I feel like Trevor is pulling away, I want to drag him closer. I reach out to touch his hand on the steering wheel.

"I'll call you tonight after this emergency is over, if you want."

"No, don't worry." Finally, the tension knotted in his shoulders loosens. "I'm gonna call Eric and Dale to come over and hang out."

Oh great. He's already made new, Molly-less plans in his head.

"Okay." Tears swell, but I blink them away.

He leans down and pecks my cheek with a kiss good-bye, but it feels robotic, like he's going through the motions. After he starts the Jeep, he revs the engine and I stand back to watch him drive down the street as he abandons me again in a cloud of exhaust.

· · ·

"They're burnt. We have to make another batch." My nine-year-old neighbor, Claire, sits on the granite countertop in the Fenway kitchen and leans over a tin of blueberry muffins on the stove, which look like hockey pucks.

No way am I making another round of muffins. It took every fiber of my being to pour oil, eggs, and water into the bowl this last time around. "Claire, you said there were five other girls in your Girl Scout group."

"It's not Girl Scouts, Molly. It's Girl *Corps*!" Claire says, clearly exasperated.

I wave my oven mitt over the surviving muffins. "Well, whatever it is, there's a dozen muffins here that aren't burnt."

"No." She smiles, her front teeth crowding her mouth in an overbite. "I only see eight that aren't burnt, not twelve."

I clench my jaws. Claire is annoying me, and Trevor hasn't answered my WISH I WERE W/U NOW text. He's probably with Dale and Eric, plotting our breakup.

I need to calm down. Not jump to conclusions. I take a deep breath and look at Claire's smooth china-doll face. "Fine, you win. But there's still enough here for each girl."

Satisfied, she nods, her blond ponytail swaying behind her head. A red Girl Corps cape wraps around her shoulders. Combined with her pajama shorts and matching fuzzy pink T-shirt, it makes a childlike fashion statement.

I've known Claire since the day she was brought home from the hospital swaddled in a pink blanket. When she was a baby, I'd visit her right after school every day, as if she were a puppy I couldn't wait to hold and tickle. Now Dede pays me to babysit Claire, but I always feel guilty for getting paid to spend time with her. Even so, it's nice to have a paying job to supplement my meager twenty-dollar-a-week allowance.

"We should get you to bed soon," I tell her.

"Why, so you can call your *boyfriend*?" she croons.

"Claire, that's personal, okay?"

"What should we do now?" She perks up. "Are you gonna go on MySpace? I'll watch."

Clueless, I tell you. "No, MySpace isn't for little kids, okay? Bedtime."

"I'm not little, and it's only eight-thirty. Let's play a game." My babysitting stints with Claire always involve games, probably because our relationship was built on peekaboo and patty-cake.

I motion to Claire to come down from the countertop. "I know you think it's early, but your mom said she wanted you in bed by eight for that walking thing you have tomorrow. I've already let you stay up past that."

"It's the muscular dystrophy walkathon, silly! Let's count my money!" Claire jumps down from her perch and I trudge behind her as she runs upstairs to her room. At least we're headed in the right direction. I'll have to bribe her to sleep, I'm sure of it.

Within the lavender walls of her room, Claire sits on her purple satin bedspread, a tally sheet, checks, and a stack of cash set out before her. "You're going to sponsor me, right, Molly?"

"Of course." I gather up her things and put them on her desk. Then I turn on her bedside lamp and flip off the ceiling light. "I just don't have my money right now. I'll give it to you tomorrow." Bribe time. "Claire?"

"Yeah?"

"I was going to give you five dollars, but I'll give you *ten* if you go to sleep right now."

Her eyebrows dip in suspicion. "Will you give me the money tonight?"

Kids these days are so paranoid! "I'll run over to my house for the money after your mom gets home, okay? It will be here when you wake up. Now get in bed."

"Shouldn't I brush my teeth?"

I'm not usually this neglectful, I'm really not, but I want Claire to get to bed so I can resume my focus on Trevor. "Your teeth look perfect. Here, get in bed."

Claire snuggles under her covers and I take her polka-dot sheet and wipe her teeth with it. "My granddad says this is how he used to brush his teeth in Ireland when he was a wee lad." Claire grins, then opens wide while I wipe each of her front teeth with a corner of the sheet.

"Will you read to me?" she asks when we're finished with our teeth-wiping protocol.

"*Claire.*"

"It's what helps me fall asleep."

"Will you go to sleep if I do?"

She makes an X over her heart with her pointer finger. "Cross my heart and hope to die."

I sigh. "All right. I'll read for five minutes."

"Twenty."

Man, give an inch and this is what happens.

"Six." Urgh!

"Ten."

"Fine!" I say through gritted teeth. "What do you want me to read?"

"This." Claire leans over her white bedside table and grabs a red book. Its cover reads *Girl Corps Handbook* inside an embossed silver heart.

"A handbook?"

"Yep," Claire says, and pulls the sheets up to her chin. "From the beginning."

I sit on the edge of the satiny bed, so slick I slide down and have to prop myself up again. "Close your eyes, Claire." She squints them shut and I start reading.

Picture this: It's 1952. Two young girls—Lila and Frances Larson of Yakima Valley, Washington— bend underneath apple trees in their family's or- chards. Their three brothers sit in the trees above, picking apples from branches, while Lila and Frances have to pick up the fallen fruit because, as their father tells them, "Climbing trees is for boys, not girls."

The younger sister, Frances, tells Lila, "Why can't we climb trees? Why can't we do what our brothers do? It's not fair! I hate being a girl. Girls don't get to do anything fun."

Her sister didn't answer for a long time; then Lila said, "We'll change that."

More than fifty years later, the changes Lila and Frances made live on in the organization they founded, the Girl Corps.

I had assumed Girl Corps was like the Girl Scouts. But it's not. There are no badges to earn (isn't that, like, half the fun?). Girl Corps is more about girls "being proud of who they are" and "personal victories."

The founders, Lila and Frances Larson, intended Girl Corps to be a place where girls could focus on improving the world, starting with themselves.

"We believe," says the all-knowing voice in the introductory letter to parents, "that if girls start with themselves—their thoughts, their dreams, their questions—then they are better able to reach outside of themselves to help and understand others. Girl Corps starts with the individual and her voice."

Claire has finally fallen asleep next to me, a dot of drool puddled on her pillow. I look up to her ceiling, which shimmers with glow-in-the-dark stick-on stars. I have lots of questions, but I'm not sure what happened to my dreams. I want to go to Ireland one day. I want to stay with Trevor. Are these my only dreams?

Maybe I should have joined Girl Corps when I was

Claire's age, instead of signing up for Jump Rope Club with Nessa. All we had were stupid "Pump and Jump" T-shirts instead of cool capes. No way did we make the world a better place by jumping rope. And it didn't teach me anything about—what was it again?—oh yeah, my voice. I reach down toward the end of Claire's bedpost, where she draped her cape. It's smooth to the touch.

"Molly?"

I jump from the side of Claire's bed at Dede's whisper behind me. "I didn't mean to startle you." Dede pokes her head farther inside the doorway. "You must not have heard me come in."

I look at the Hello Kitty wall clock. It's almost ten. My God, I totally lost track of time reading this book. I set it down on Claire's nightstand, twist her bedside light off, and tiptoe out into the hallway. "I thought you'd be home later."

"Well, we didn't have our usual long wait in the ER." She glances over at Claire. "Gimme a sec?"

Dede hovers over Claire's bed, straightens her covers, and leans down to kiss her forehead. Daddy and the uncles have tucked me into bed my entire life, but the sight of Dede's softness toward her daughter hurts, because I know I was cheated out of those same goodnight kisses from my own mother.

Dede tiptoes back into the hallway and closes Claire's door behind her.

"Is your mom okay?" I ask. Our shoulders rub as we walk down the stairway.

"Just a bump on the head, but they did a CAT scan. Robert stayed behind with her in case she wakes and is disoriented. The doctor said it could be a concussion." At the bottom of the stairs she reaches out and gives me a hug. "Thank you, Molly. I appreciate your last-minute help."

"No problem."

At the doorway, Dede turns, her eyes on the droopy side of tired. "Would it be okay if I paid you tomorrow? I need to get cash."

"Sure." I reach for the door handle.

"Thanks a bunch, Molly."

"G'night." I slip out the door, where the full moon gives an eerie sense of light to what's normally dark. I look over to my barren driveway next door. The men are no doubt at the Banshee.

I'd text Trevor again, but I don't want to bug him. He's probably still hanging out with his friends, enjoying guy time playing Texas Hold 'Em poker and belching the alphabet.

The spikes of grass blades poke my ankles as I walk onto our crisp lawn. My phone vibrates in my pocket. Callback number: Vanessa's.

"Hey, Mollers." Her mouth is full of food. Whatever she's eating, it's got massive crunch. "I'm surprised you picked up."

"What's up, Ness?"

"Well, just got off work. I was driving over to Jasmine's house and passed by Loverboy's place." There is a rustling in the background, and I know she's dipping her hand into a bag of chips. "The lights are all off, but his Jeep is parked in front of the garage, so I thought you guys might be . . . *indisposed*."

Shouldn't there be the equivalent of a frat party going on at Trevor's house?

My heart pounds so hard that I put my hand on my chest. "I'm not at Trevor's house. I had to babysit Claire tonight."

Now the silence is on Vanessa's end. "Oh. Well, maybe he went to sleep early."

I want to tell her that Trevor is supposed to be in the middle of some type of male-bonding ritual, but I don't want to admit that something sketchy might be going on. Still, this theory of mine has a stranglehold on my neck, and I have to prove it wrong or risk certain suffocation.

"I gotta go," I say brusquely before hanging up. Then I run and grab my rusted bike from the side of my house and launch myself toward Trevor's, because walking won't get me there fast enough.

8

My lame Huffy cruiser creeps up the Everest slope of Marlborough Hill toward Trevor's house. Sweat droplets bead on my face in the humid night air once I reach the crest of the hill. Street signs blur as I whiz toward 4599 Kensington Street, where I clumsily steer into the driveway.

I stay perched on my bike to catch my breath.

Trevor's Jeep is in front of the garage, just like Vanessa said it was. No sign of Eric's Acura or Dale's truck. The porch light is off, and so is every other light in the house. Except in the den, where a dim glow seeps from the blinds. I check my watch: 10:34 p.m. My stomach becomes a jar of frantic moths. A great sense of foreboding surrounds me, but it doesn't shake me enough to send me home. Instead, I lean my bike against a hulky tree and tiptoe across Trevor's lawn.

The short skirt I put on earlier becomes a bit less of a good idea as I straddle the spiky hedge (yeow!) and lurch toward the den window to sneak a quick peek. I balance my elbows on the window frame, and peer through a fracture in the blinds.

Oh.

Oh, no.

Felicia Mitchell's golden ex-girlfriend hair fans out over the sofa pillows. Trevor lies next to her. She presses her body closer to his; he rests his hand on her tight stomach. The hammer in my chest begins to pound violently; my head throbs with heat.

They're kissing on his sofa, the sofa where he kisses me. I struggle to breathe. My stomach contorts into duck-and-cover. I squeeze my eyes shut. "This can't be happening."

But then I open them, and it is. Trevor's hand brushes a lock of Felicia's hair away from her face and he caresses her cheek: The urgent kisses should bother me the most, but it's the tenderness between them that causes me to detonate.

I pound my fist against the windowpane.

Dull thud.

Startled, Trevor rolls off Felicia and in a quick move reaches over to flick off the table lamp. Between thwacks, I track moving shadows inside the room.

Two shadows.

Thump!

Then none.

Thud!

My body shakes uncontrollably, a thousand earth-quakes inside. I've lived my entire life within earshot of my dad and uncles hammering nails into wooden floor planks, but my fist is a sad hammer: *Thunk! Splut! Thwuck!*

Molly, I love you.

I said it back. *I love you, too, Trevor.* Words that had melted inside my mouth like morsels of silky chocolate.

I hear footsteps.

"Molly?" A disheveled Trevor has me cornered. I remain still, like Vinny the gecko, trapped inside the terrarium in Trevor's room. My hands grip the window frame like suction cups. My body adheres to the sand-paper stucco-sided house.

"What are you doing?" he asks. How can he be so calm when the world feels like it's tilting?

My hands slip, but I land on my own two flip-flopped feet, then turn to face Trevor. "You lied to me." I stand behind the hedge, tearful and trembling in the heat that keeps rising.

Trevor wiggles a hand through his croppy hair. His brown eyes, once twinkling, suddenly cast a dark spotlight. "Look, she just showed up on my door-step."

"No"—my voice tightens—"she was on your couch. Kissing you. You kissed her. You told me it was *over* between you two." The words tumble out. "I *believed* you."

Trevor sighs. I thought I knew his face by heart, but a crease I've never seen before stretches across his forehead. "You know I've moved on, but she's having a tough time with all of this, Molly."

"What do you think *I'm* having?" I shriek, and hurdle over to Trevor so I can pummel his chest with my fists.

For the past twelve weeks I have lived on the small island of this boy. I've sacrificed time with my best friend to spend most of my waking hours waiting for Trevor to call.

I walk backward, away from him. Tears spill down my cheeks. When I turn to leave, Trevor grabs my shoulders, forcing me to look into his cheating eyes. "Shhh, Molly, calm down." He pulls me into his arms to stop me from running.

I reach to push him away, but Trevor bends down and whispers, "I don't love her, Molly. I love you."

What? I want to believe him, I do. My hands stretch out to block his face, but he rests his chin in my palms. I should want to reach down his throat and pluck out his heart, but for this split second, I'm stuck.

The distance he created earlier today is gone. We're close again. I relax my fingers. My thumb traces the inside of his hoop earring.

Trevor looks beyond me toward the den window.

With his head still in my hands, I turn to see a silhouetted Felicia peek out from the blinds.

"It's over!" I shove him away, except my thumb gets caught inside his earring and yanks the loop from his lobe.

Trevor howls and clamps his ear.

"Are you okay?" I squeak. "I didn't mean to—"

"Are you psycho?" Blood seeps between his fingers.

I snap and reel back, stunned. "You cheated on me!"

I slip the earring from my thumb, flick it into the grass, and run to recover my bike.

While trying to mount it, I lose my footing. The sharp-edged pedal scrapes deep along my calf, but that doesn't stop me. I jam my foot down and pump fast and faster down the never-ending street.

Tears stream sideways and burrow inside my ears. I look to see if he's followed me, half wishing that the headlights of his Jeep will appear so at least I'll know he meant what he said, that he loved me. But he's not there. The image of Trevor tenderly touching Felicia on the sofa instant-replays in my head. Suddenly, no matter how hard I pedal, I can't tear my thoughts away from that snapshot.

The bowl of cornflakes I ate for dinner rises up in my throat, the Pepto-Bismol close behind. I brake at one of the many cookie-cutter Spanish-style homes on perfectly manicured lawns, lean over my handlebars, and puke into a bed of white roses.

A sensor porch light flares and I make a quick

getaway. When I reach the top of Marlborough Hill, I stop, my sour breath too fast to catch. Blood drips from the wound on my calf.

I look down the hill at my neighborhood. The "other" side of town, South Hilldale, where our old houses look like the dead snakeskins the newer, bigger homes in North Hilldale slinked out of. I launch my bike down the hill and farther away from Trevor. My hair flies behind me like a red feathery wing.

At the corner of my street, my legs reverse and jam on the brakes. I look toward home. A streetlight flickers above me, and in its eerie strobe I flash back to the days when Daddy propped me up on his lap, where he'd guide my fingers over the keys of Buttons until his bellows squeezed out a song.

Daddy's blue eyes would look into my own, and he'd tell me in his Irish-accented voice, "Molly, be wise and wide. Guard yourself like a leprechaun would protect his treasure."

Unlike the wee men of Ireland, I don't know how to speak in riddles. I never asked Trevor to leap over a rainbow for a kiss.

Maybe the real treasure is the stuff you offer from inside yourself—the feelings, the time you spend thinking about another person and worrying whether they feel the same—those are the golden things that expose you and make you hope for something bigger in return.

One minute you're crazy in love, announcing it to

the boy who has your heart in his hands. *I love you:* words that make you feel more naked than nakedness itself.

The next minute, you're stranded under a lamppost, realizing that he lied, he doesn't love you, and you're not getting anything from him. Not even the gold he managed to steal away from you.

9

It's muggy in my house, so I stay out on the porch. Blotches of dried blood cover my calf. I tighten my eyelids and beckon the ice queen inside me, beg her to shut off the faucet. She normally lets me down, and tonight is no exception.

I pluck my phone out of my skirt pocket and call Nessa, but after two rings, I get her voice mail: "Call me, Ness." I can't say anything else because my throat closes up.

A lone cricket chirps in the yard under the olive tree. Tears drip down my face. I intertwine my fingers and clench my eyes shut again.

Saint Brigid, Mary of Ireland,
Ask for us all today
The courage to do God's bidding

Whatever the world may say,
The grace to be strong—

I can't remember the rest.

"Please, help me, Saint Brigid. It hurts." Eyes open.

I hear nothing but the cricket. I rub my eyes against my knobby knees. My own saint won't return my calls. She's probably disgusted with me, and I can hardly blame her because I don't pray much and my skirt is too short and I don't know how to use my mother's sapphire blue rosary beads. "Mom? Are *you* there?"

"What's wrong?" A small voice startles me. I turn to my right and near the bottom step of the porch is a familiar little girl in a bright red cape.

"Jesus, Claire!" I catch my breath. "You scared the crap out of me."

"You shouldn't use swearwords."

"Well, you shouldn't sneak up behind people like that."

"Why are you crying and who were you talking to?"

I wipe my cheeks with my wrist. "Shouldn't you be in bed? You were asleep earlier." She holds the glossy walkathon sponsor sheet in one hand and a stubby pencil in the other.

"I woke up and couldn't go back to sleep. I saw you." She points up to her bedroom window. "From my window seat." Uninvited, Claire sits next to me on the porch step; her bare toes curl against the cement. "So, why are you crying?"

"I'm not crying!" I wipe away more evidence. "Go home, Claire. Please."

"Well"—she leans in closer for a better look—"you look like you've been crying. Plus I *heard* you crying."

I pull back. "You're too young to be outside by yourself this time of night."

"You said you'd sponsor me in the walkathon. You didn't leave me the money."

Twinge of guilt. I did say I would, but seriously, I wasn't thinking about the stupid money when I left Claire's house. Still, this is bad timing. "I can't give anything right now, okay?"

She pauses a moment. "But Ms. Rhondi says that when you give, you get."

Whoever Ms. Rhondi is, she obviously has her head up her arse, pardon my Irish.

"Well, Claire," I say, suddenly feeling mean and willing to burst bubbles, "it's not true." My face becomes a furnace. "Sometimes when you give, you get betrayed, you lose, and there's no getting back what you gave. *Ever!*" I bring my face closer to her. "You get that?"

Claire recoils in fear and nods. She recovers way too quickly and whips the pledge sheet into my face again. "But I need the money. Ten bucks. You said."

Ergh! I can't take this right now. "Shut up!"

Claire's chin quivers.

Oh, no.

She sniffles and stands up.

"Claire—" I get up and step toward her. "Please don't go." A tear races down her cheek. "I'll donate, okay?"

She whimpers.

No wonder Saint Brigid didn't hear me. She's blocked all calls from me because I'm a disgusting human being. "Claire?" I rest my hand on her shoulder. She looks up at me and I wipe her tears away with my thumb. "I'm sorry. I'll donate. Fifteen dollars, okay?"

She keeps crying. Did I aim too low? "Twenty?"

She moans and the tears keep coming.

"Thirty dollars?"

Now she's wailing! Dede is going to hear, and so will the whole neighborhood. "Claire!" I kneel down and look up at her face, brush aside a stray blond hair that's escaped its ponytail holder. "I've saved one hundred dollars. I'll give that to you, okay? Just please, stop crying."

You better hear me now, Saint Brigid!

"Will you do the walkathon, too?" she whines.

"Yes, I'll walk with you. I'll give you a hundred dollars. I'll even let you play with my phone next time I babysit."

"Really?" Claire sniffs, winding down.

I nod. "Yeah."

"When?"

Oh geez. "Soon, okay? Now let's get you inside."

"No," she says, not budging. "You said you'd give

me the money tonight." She tucks her chin down and purses her lips.

I know an immovable object when I see one.

"Fine." I disappear into the house and dash upstairs to my room. From my panty drawer I pull out an old green soccer sock where I keep my cash, and fumble for my hundred dollars: money that was originally set aside for taking Trevor out to dinner at Mona Lisa's for his birthday on November fifth. Just three weeks from now. He loves Italian food.

I'm not sure I'll ever be able to eat pizza again without bursting into tears. Or puking.

I fly down the stairs two at a time. Outside, Claire waits on the porch. "Here," I say. I grab her hands and plop the crumpled bills into them.

She releases a smile. "Thanks, Molly!"

I put my arm around her shoulder and lead her down the porch and over into her yard. "Bye, Claire," I say, and gently coax her up the steps toward her front door.

"See you tomorrow!" She waves back and slips inside.

After I tilt my bike against the side of the house, I trudge through the front door again into the darkened hallway, this time taking notice of the print of the Virgin Mary. Next to her hangs the oval portrait of my three uncles, Daddy, Granddad, and me, age seven. I can't see the picture so well, only the outline, but I have it memorized. We're all holding our musical instruments on our knees.

I reach out and trace the silhouette of the girl with the accordion on her lap and a toothless smile on her face. That's when life was simple, I guess. When a Friday night revolved around pressing the right buttons on the accordion and helping it wheeze out a tune that made you wonder if the hills of Ireland are as green as they appear in the pictures you've seen. Back then it wasn't ever about a boy or the breaking of a heart.

I don't remember falling asleep, but in the powdery hour of morning, when clouds and dreams crisscross, the squeak of the twisting doorknob wakes me.

"Daddy?" I pretended I had been sleeping instead of crying when he came in after midnight last night and checked on me when he got home. Tears activate the panic button in Daddy. It's best to hold back.

The window-framed image of Felicia and Trevor on his couch flashes in my mind, then punches like a fist into my stomach. I fumble for my glasses on the night-stand.

"Good morning," says Claire. Her fuzzy pink paja-mas from last night have been replaced by denim shorts and a pale yellow tank top. Her little red cape is intact. She sidles closer to my bed. "I didn't know you still wear glasses."

"I can't sleep with my contact lenses in." I rub my eyes. "What are you doing here?" I sit up on my elbows; my body feels sore, listless. The fiery red digits on my clock flare out at me.

She's got to be kidding.

"Claire."

Her eyes dance around my room. "Your room is *so* cool. I wish I could live in an attic." She stops at the clothesline of Barbies hung over my curtains. "What did you do to those Barbies?"

"Claire, it's six-thirty in the morning." I don't think I've slept at all but have only nodded in and out of being awake and in a zombielike dream state. My eyes sting with the hangover of last night's crying. And what about Trevor's ear? Maybe he had to go to the hospital. I wish I didn't care.

Claire gawks at the Barbies that Nessa and I made over back in fifth grade. Specifically, she's gaping at Mohawk Barbie, who we adorned with Sharpie tattoos and tiny beaded piercings.

"Claire?"

She turns, but not without gulping in a stare at Mod Barbie and Beatnik Ken, both sporting berets fashioned from Guinness bottle caps. "Your grandpa told me I could come up here and get you. We're leaving in fifteen minutes. You know, for the walkathon?"

"Right." I moan. "The walkathon." I don't know how I'm going to get out of bed.

She walks toward my desk and now fixates on the

blurry phone-camera pictures I've printed out of Trevor and me. Our faces pressed together in a close-up; a profile of Trevor I took while he was driving, a sliver of sunshine glinting off his sunglasses.

Claire scrunches her nose and points at the bulletin board. "You sure have a lot of pictures of Trevor."

Yes. Yes I do. And even though they're of horrible quality, the sight of them is enough to bring back the tears, so I look away.

Claire needs to leave, because I've got an appointment with a mental breakdown. I lumber out of bed and lead her toward the door. "Now you go so I can get ready."

"But you're dressed."

She's right. I never bothered to put on pajamas. "I need to change, okay?"

"I'll wait for you." I open the door and nudge Claire, like I'm shooing a chicken out of a coop.

From behind the closed door she says, "See you in a bit!"

I grab my cell from my nightstand.

Texts: zero.

Voice mails: zero.

Missed calls: zero.

Attempted contact or apology from Trevor: zero.

They are the kind of zeroes that seem like they might add up to something. Something more than zero.

I wonder why Vanessa didn't return my message,

and press speed dial. "Mollers?" The loud music in the background blares.

"Where are you?"

"I'm driving to work. You know how the Buck Stops Here loves them some Vanessa on Saturdays." Since she's had the job this past year, she's put in a full eight-hour day on Saturdays. She has to in order to pay her car insurance.

"Didn't you get my message last night?" I ask.

"No, why?" She turns off the music. "What's up? You okay?"

I walk over to my tidy desk and finger the tendrils of rust-colored hair on the mask Trevor gave me, then zoom in on the bulletin board at a picture of me and Trevor at the beach this summer. His arm wraps around my waist, just above the band of my purple bikini. "I caught Trevor with Felicia Mitchell last night."

"He cheated on you with *Felicia*?"

"Yes." I rip the picture from the board, wad it up in my hand, and toss it into the trash can with the rough draft of my history report on Guyana. I tell Nessa the details and how I accidentally ripped out his earring.

"No. Way," Vanessa says in disbelief. "That is so hard-core! He's lucky you didn't yank something else off and throw it in the bushes. And don't go beating yourself up about this, either. He's a jackass."

I moan. "It'd be so much easier if I could hate him right now."

"I'm gonna come by after work. We'll figure something out to cheer you up."

"Thanks, Ness."

"You know me love you." She says it in our signature cavewoman voice.

"Me love you, too."

I press my back against the wall and absorb the panorama of the remaining Trevor pictures. I should want to burn them, but I have the urge to rip them from the board, reclaim the two I just crumpled up, and clutch them all to my chest.

Under my bed there's a Vans shoe box full of e-mails between us. I want to riffle through that box, too. What is it about me that I would consider a dangerous trip down memory lane with Trevor even though I know it's going to make me feel worse? It's sick.

A metallic taste creeps over my tongue, like I've got a mouthful of nickels.

I gotta get out of here. I do.

I skip my ritual of showering, shaving, shampooing, hair-straightening, and eyelash curling. Within seven minutes, I've got my contacts in and my mass of red hair tied back in a ponytail, and have slipped into a pair of shorts, a black tank, and flip-flops. Some orange juice to revive me and I'll be on my way.

I clip down the steps from the attic to the second-floor landing, where the wood beneath me changes from maple to dark oak. Daddy's open bedroom door reveals his crisply made bed.

"Morning, Molly B." I turn to the source of the soft

voice. In the bedroom across from Daddy's, Uncle Rourke sits at the edge of his mattress, hunched over the laces of his faded leather work boots. A huge poster of the band Thin Lizzy stretches across the wall behind him between two towering bookshelves, the lead singer's Afro sprouting up toward the sky.

"Hey, Uncle Rourke."

"We missed you last night at the Banshee."

"Did Granddad and Clem win the Battle of the Bands?" In the midst of my own drama, I'd forgotten about Bangers, Beans, and Battle of the Bands over at the Banshee.

"Yup. I swear those lads will never be beat."

"Well, I'll see you later." I wave, grab the smooth banister, and jog down another flight of steps to the entry hall, where oak transitions to a deeper shade of cherrywood. Uncle Murph's voice booms from the kitchen. "Smells like you burned the eggs again, Garrett!"

I walk through the kitchen doorway into the workday-morning routine of Daddy and the uncles, where they become a blur of blue jeans and button-up work shirts. It's not rare for them to work on Saturdays or even Sundays.

"Dammit!" Uncle Garrett lurches from the stove and crouches over his hand.

"It's an iron skillet, you gimp!" shouts Uncle Murph. "You need an oven mitt." He scoots his chair out from the kitchen table, where Daddy and Granddad eat and absorb newspaper headlines.

"Morning." I've pulled myself together—posture! posture!—and walk full throttle toward the cup cabinet, where mismatched glasses and labeled coffee mugs are stacked like Leaning Tower of Pisa models. I make a safe grab for a pint glass.

Uncle Murph peers into Uncle Garrett's skillet. "Hey, Mol. Your poor uncle Gar can't manage to make an egg."

Uncle Garrett holds his wrist and shakes his hand. "Hump off, Murph, I'm in pain."

"Go eat your toast and butter, you ninny. I'll make you some decent eggs."

Uncle Garrett offers me a wink on his way to the table. "Got out of that one."

"Well, Molly," says Daddy. My back is to him as I open the refrigerator. "What gets you up at the crack of dawn on a Saturday?"

"I'm doing a charity walk with Claire." I grab the almost empty carton of orange juice from the top shelf, where it sits next to an immense jar of pickled hard-boiled eggs, a family favorite.

When I turn, Daddy halts his attack on the enormous bowl of oatmeal in front of him and eyes me, his freshly showered head of thinning hair combed neatly to the side. "Something wrong there, Mol?" This causes all the men to turn their attention toward me.

Bah! I'm not crying; my face doesn't feel red. I thought I was doing a good job sucking in my misery. "Nope. I'm fine."

"You don't look yourself," says Daddy. He plants an elbow on the table. "Does it have anything to do with that boy, Trevor?"

"No," I insist, and swirl my orange juice in my glass to watch the pulpy whirlpool. "It's just my contacts are bugging me. I didn't sleep well, either." I shrug. "No big deal."

They continue to stare. "I'm fine, okay?"

Daddy scoots his chair out from the table. "I don't believe you. What happened? That boy give you lip about the talk we had with him?"

I still don't even know everything they said. There's a knock at the door, which makes me grateful for Claire. "I gotta go." I set my glass in the sink and rush out of the kitchen.

But Daddy follows me into the hall. "Are *you* upset about me talking to Trevor?"

I turn back to him, shocked a bit that he thinks he's done wrong here. "No, Daddy, it's not that." I'm not thrilled about Daddy talking to Trevor, but at least I know he did it because he cares.

I could tell him right now about what I saw last night, what happened. This is a man who would do anything for me.

But if he knew what happened last night, he'd only be angry that I got hurt. "I've got some stuff to work out in my head, Daddy."

"You want to talk about it?"

"No, not now. Just please, don't worry." I stand

on tiptoe and kiss his smooth-shaven cheek. "I've got to go."

"We'll be home this afternoon, okay, love?" Daddy calls after me.

"Okay. Bye!" I shout back as I walk out of the house.

I've spent my entire life trying to protect Daddy from seeing me upset. He's had a hard time of it, losing my mother, working long hours. There's no sense in upsetting him over something I know no one can fix. Not even me.

Outside, the air feels warm, no matter that it's barely seven in the morning. The heat wave continues. The Fenway car idles at the curb: a gargantuan shiny black vehicle with tinted windows that undoubtedly is responsible for depleting a good portion of the ozone layer.

I take a deep breath and step up into the open passenger door. Dede smiles from behind designer sunglasses that look more like protective eyewear for use with a blowtorch. Her sleeveless black spandex top and yoga pants show off her tight body—a result of her dedication to Pilates.

"Hi, Molly!" Claire waves from the back with the foil-covered tray of what I assume to be the unburnt muffins from last night.

"You are such a generous heart!" Dede shrieks, and

leans over to hug me before I can fasten my seat belt. She doesn't let go. "One hundred dollars. Oh, it's just so good of you, Molly. And you walking today? It means so much to Claire." She squeezes more tightly. "This is so wonderful!" Even though I sort of wish she would let go and drive, I can't help absorbing her compliments against the backdrop of rejection.

"There aren't enough teens like you, are there?" I take the question as rhetorical. She pulls away from our hug. "Ooh, look at that," she says, pointing at the clock in the overcrowded console. "Time to roll!"

What kind of teen am I exactly? Oh yeah, the kind who'd consider messing around with her boyfriend just to keep him. I can't believe I'm that stupid.

Dede drives us through residential South Hilldale, where most of the lawns remain riddled with dead patches of grass, battle wounds from a hot summer that still lingers in mid-October. A few eager souls have already carved pumpkins.

"Is your mom doing better?" I ask.

"Yep. Claire and I are heading over to see her after the walkathon. Until then, Robert's in charge."

She turns toward Hilldale's downtown, which is dotted with what Granddad calls mom-and-pop shops: Bookends, a used-book store; Joseph's Pharmacy, where Aunt Tip asked Joe for guidance on what kind of maxi pad we should purchase the day I started my period (I still can't look him in the eye).

We pass the Banshee's Wake, where Aunt Tipper will unlock the black door in a few hours, at eleven. At this hour, it looks out of place. As if it were shipped over here in pieces—thick chunks of wood and stained glass—carted from Ireland like the Statue of Liberty from France.

Dede turns left into Eucalyptus Park. Gravel crunches underneath the tires as she steers into the not-so-crowded parking lot.

About half a football field away, a half dozen or so red-capeleted girls, led by a large woman, lunge their legs and stretch their arms in a warm-up. A few parents, brightly dressed in running shorts, stand off to the side.

"Ready, ladies?" Dede asks, but Claire has already jumped out of the car and sprinted toward the group. "She's just so excited about you being here, Molly."

I'm out of place here. Girl Corps is for little girls. Not big girls. Not me.

"Molly!" Claire shouts as she runs back toward the car. Four girls stand behind her, smiling up at me as I join them.

If there were a variety pack of girls that one could pluck from a supermarket shelf, this would be it. Several ethnicities are represented: Asian, African American, Latina, and Caucasian. They're unified by red capes and white sneakers.

Claire turns to them like she's a museum tour guide and I'm the display, and says, "This is Molly."

The girls become a small mob of ponytailed paparazzi who buzz around me.

"Molly!" the one with the black pin-strait hair says.

The girl with the gorgeous mocha-colored skin and thick thatch of brown spiral curls shouts, "Hi, Molly!"

"How old are you, Molly?" asks a girl with the most velvety brown eyes I've ever seen. "Do you have a dog?" she adds. Totally random.

It should be made clear that I have no desire to be a role model. I don't want some raving-lunatic mother to blame me for the rotting of her child's family values if I fail to be perfect—which is likely.

But I have to admit that these girls are making me feel pretty pop star right now. I'm wrapped in their arms and I don't even know them.

Compliments whiz through the air.

"You're so pretty!"

"I like your blue nail polish!" This said by a girl who is the victim of early orthodontia, her mouth a jumble of wire and brackets.

"Is that your real hair?"

As I stand embraced in their whirlpool of chatter, another, less enthusiastic voice thunderclaps from the edge of the lawn. "Girls, time to assemble!"

The girls quickly skitter back to the picnic table, and I feel the abrupt loss of their presence—like when I go to a party and Nessa slithers off with someone and I'm left to stand alone amid people who gyrate to loud music that has an exaggerated, fuzzy bass beat. Talk about awkward.

Directly in front of me stands the source of the voice that took the girls away from me: a tall woman in a red satin cape who looks like something out of a fractured Mother Goose rhyme.

This must be Rhondi. With obvious reluctance, I walk toward her, both magnetized and frightened. She's quite large, not obese but very lumberjack-like, rivaling the eucalyptus trees surrounding the park. She's probably carrying two hundred plus pounds of muscle. Her short salt-and-pepper hair is on the verge of spiky.

She doesn't wear a red capelet like the girls. No, she's sporting a huge red magician's cape that's covered with what look like fake diamonds. From what I read in Claire's *Girl Corps Handbook* last night, there are no badges to earn in Girl Corps, but the jewel flair must mean something important, or at least signify rank.

"Dede just told me that you'll be walking with us today?" My heartbeat escalates at Rhondi's stare, which has me wondering if she's got X-ray vision. Her dark brown eyes can probably see the Lycra fibers of my panties and the bent underwire of my bra and would deem them improper.

"I can leave if it's not okay," I say, half hoping this will give me an out.

"You don't need to leave. I just want to make sure you're committed to the walk."

"Yeah." I nod. She seems uncomfortably super-serious about this.

Rhondi bends toward me. She smells like baby

powder, but this makes her no less intimidating. "Please be mindful of your neckline. These girls notice everything."

Gulp. For the most part, Rhondi's cape covers up her own boobs, but I'm guessing from the hemispheric bulges underneath she's a double E.

Ashamed in my tank top, I cross my arms over my chest. In my defense, it's hot, the same kind of heat that rushes out of the oven when I peer into it to get a whiff of Uncle Murph's potato bread. If Rhondi knew me, she'd know that I'm in no way trying to score an ogle from the opposite sex or draw attention to my B cups.

"We're going to get started here in a few minutes." Rhondi escorts me to the girls at a picnic table that's scattered with paperwork, juice boxes, and the tray of blueberry muffins.

I suddenly feel remorse about having been too lazy to make another batch. The growl in my stomach reminds me that I didn't grab something to eat this morning, but I'm afraid to reach for a muffin in case Rhondi should decide I'm not worthy and bite off my hand.

A girl with dark hair and aggressively trimmed bangs sits at the table. "Hello," I say. She glowers in response.

"Up, up, Sophia," Rhondi says to her. When Rhondi turns, Sophia glares at her behind her back. Scary, but at least there might be a rebel among us who doesn't immediately step into place at the command of Rhondi. Already, I feel slight admiration for Sophia.

"Okay, girls," Rhondi says. "We've got six hours ahead of us." *Six hours?* "Parents?" Dede and the two other women stop chatting. "You know our pit stops and time zones." They nod.

Time zones? *Six* hours? Even though my legs are twice as long as the shortest girl here, I'm really starting to wish I could climb back in bed and listen to a steady stream of sad songs to feed my heartbreak. But no—instead I'm doing the Girl Corps Death March.

During the first fifteen minutes of our walk, Claire makes sure I'm introduced to each girl: Hatsuku, Ayisha, Emily, Maribel, and Sophia. Each one of them beams after I repeat her name, except for Sophia, who is an expert eye roller.

The first hour, we trek the bark-lined perimeter of the park and my feet endure sharp pokes from the splintering shards of timber.

Then my phone rings and my heart leaps, hoping it's Trevor. He already said sorry and I love you last night. It's not that I want to hear any specific words as much as I want to know he's making an effort to reach me, even though I probably wouldn't reach back.

It rings again. "No electronic devices!" booms Rhondi. Geesh, talk about a control freak. She keeps walking full speed ahead and begins to hum a song I can't quite name, which, as off-key as it may be, kind of puts me at ease. At least she likes music.

I fall to the back of the group, then reach down to turn off my ringer and steal a glimpse of Vanessa's call-back number, not Trevor's. I'm disgusted with myself for wanting him to call, but the fact that it wasn't him makes me walk even slower.

Ayisha falls back with me, her hair a thriving mass of brown corkscrews sprouting over her shoulders and out into the air. "Who called you?" Claire and Hatsuku clump next to her like petals trying to reattach to a flower.

I pat my phone in my pocket. "My friend."

"Vanessa?" Claire seems pleased that she knows me well enough to guess.

I nod.

Hatsuku brings a pinky finger up to her mouth and nibbles on the remaining stub of nail; a smile creeps out from the huge globe of her face. "Claire said your boyfriend is really cute."

I stop walking and the three girls follow my cue. I don't have a boyfriend. It's simple, like the story line out of one of those easy reader books from my childhood:

Molly loves Trevor.
Does Trevor love Molly?
No, because Trevor kisses Felicia.
Bad Trevor!

Uh-oh, Molly is hurt.
Trevor loves Felicia now.
Bye-bye, Molly!
The end.

I feel dizzy all of a sudden. I hate this story, but I know it's going to keep telling itself over and over in my head in more detail. How I want him to chase me down, like my life is some cheesy soap opera. I want to burst. To scream!

"What's the matter?" Hatsuku now gnaws at her thumbnail.

Claire grabs my arm. "Did you and Trevor break up?"

"Girls!" Rhondi calls to us from about thirty feet away. Maribel sticks right to her side, and lone wolf Sophia trails them, while the four of us are obviously too far behind.

"Something wrong?"

"Sorry, Ms. Rhondi. We're coming!" shouts Claire.

"Get walking, then!" Rhondi shouts back. "We are what we do."

The four of us find our stride, but we're squished together on the sidewalk. If our arms were looped together, I'd look like Dorothy with her trio of friends in *The Wizard of Oz*. It's obvious that there is little concern for my personal space. Claire climbs back into the subject. "So did you and Trevor break up, then?"

"Yes." It's a short word, but my voice quavers as I say it. Admitting I don't have a boyfriend is accepting that it's over between Trevor and me. I've spent so much time worrying about losing him. And just like that, it's over. Expired. The gravity of this is like placing a brick on top of a house of cards.

Hatsuku, who walks on the other side of Ayisha, leans around her from the edge of our line. Her face is perfectly round like a full moon. "Did he dump you?"

"*Dump* me?" Dumped. Flung away. Cheated on. It's all the same, isn't it? Immediately, my stomach collapses and I can feel it fall, like it's tumbling down a staircase. I'm not sure who dumped who here, but I definitely feel like I was the one cast off, and I feel even worse that the truth of it has been presented to me by a nine-year-old.

"Look, I'm fine. See?" I start walking faster and zoom past Sophia's sneer. Walk, walk, walk. Then I reach Maribel's happy-go-lucky bouncy gait, and I'm right behind our caped shepherd.

"Finally, you're walking faster." Rhondi says it over her shoulder as she picks up the pace even more. I'm not that competitive, but for some reason, I quicken my steps to keep up with her, except she centers herself more evenly on the sidewalk to ensure that I don't pass her, which is quite effective.

Fine, then. I leech on to a steady pace and I'm not going to stop. The closer I get to thinking about Trevor, the more weighed down I feel. It's better to just walk. The harder I walk, the more I concentrate on my breath and my sloppy footing, which is difficult to control in flip-flops, but not impossible.

. . .

During hour three, I'm in the back of the group. Blister formation accelerates from the rubbing of my flip-flop between my big and second toe, but I can ignore the pain because Emily has slowed down her pace to keep me company. She's the girl with braces who reminds me of a pixie-sized hippie: her long, stringy hair parts down the middle and a peace sign explodes on her orange T-shirt. She's the tiniest in the group, her arms so thin they look like saplings.

As we walk behind the others, she pulls something out of the bluest blue. "If you were on a desert island and could only bring three things with you, what would they be?" Her lips struggle to fit comfortably over the brackets of her braces.

"I have no idea, Emily," I say. She obviously doesn't know that if you can live without a mother, you can live without just about anything. "What's your answer?"

"I'd bring my Webkinz, my good-luck rock, and my Girl Journal."

"Cool," I say, without mentioning that those items probably wouldn't help her much with survival. But why ruffle her young feathers? Emily speeds up her gait to ask the same question of Sophia, who mumbles something about a generator and an iPod.

By hour four, I admit that I have a tiny speck of pride that I've walked this far without breaking down into a slumpy hump. Hatsuku runs back to me and shares her thoughts on cloud formations: "There!" she points, her pale arm unfolding into a straight line toward the sky. "That's an ostrich eating a tulip. What's it look like to you?"

I squint up at the cloud and instead of telling her what it really looks like (an anemic heart pierced with an ice pick), I say, "A white puffy prom dress on a hanger?"

"Neat!" she answers.

My feet hurt. My blisters swell.

Hour five, it's clear that sweating through a few sets of accordion playing onstage and walking from one end of Hilldale High's campus to the other isn't enough to constitute an exercise regimen. I am out of shape, in back of the group. The sandals rub relentlessly against my feet. The sun has been baking us all morning, and I forgot to put on sunscreen. Not a good mix, with my stupid fair skin.

But it's not until the sole of my flip-flop catches a raised crack on the sidewalk that I realize this is ludicrous. I'm not walking for muscular dystrophy, I'm walking to forget about Trevor. I tumble; my arms fly out, but not fast enough to prevent my mouth from pounding the pockmarked sidewalk.

My face presses against warm concrete.

Salty blood from my lip trickles into my mouth.

The entire group huddles around my crime-scene sprawl on the sidewalk in front of a mobile-home park.

I'm so exhausted, I don't even bother to get up. "Are you okay?" Rhondi asks above me.

Am I okay?

Sometimes you're asked a simple question that triggers something inside you to crackle. "No," I moan. And I mean it. Tears start to spill down my cheeks.

Rhondi crouches down farther and takes a handkerchief from her pocket, like she's prepared to wipe tears from a crying walker. I wonder for a second why she's leading these girls. I didn't catch wind that any of them belong to her. She dabs my face with the soft fabric of the hanky. "Do you think you've broken anything?"

Does a heart count? "I don't think so."

"We're going to try and get you up, okay? Girls, help me out here." Hands surround me, gently tugging and pressing until I'm coaxed into a standing position.

"Thanks," I say, blinking my moist eyes.

She nods and points to my mouth. "Your teeth look okay, it's just your lip that seems to be bleeding."

"And she's crying," says Emily, who looks like she's ready to cry herself.

"She was crying last night and this morning, too!" Claire offers. Thanks, Claire.

"It's because of her boyfriend, I bet." Very perceptive, Hatsuku. Ergh!

I quickly rub my eyes again, dab my tank top at the spot of blood on my upper lip, then lick it away.

"Her lip is growing!" Maribel shouts.

"Stay calm, Maribel," says Sophia.

Emily nods. "I fell once and my braces scraped my lip open."

"Eww, Emily!" says Ayisha.

"Should we call an ambulance, Ms. Rhondi?" asks Hatsuku.

A ride in an ambulance right now sounds appealing. Rhondi studies me for a second. "She's okay. Right, Molly?"

I don't answer and instead cast my eyes down at the pink skid marks on my feet.

"Now, girls," Rhondi says, "remember at our meeting last Thursday we learned some first-aid techniques with Nurse Todd?" *Nurse Todd?* "What kind of first aid does Molly need?" Nice that she's using me as a live specimen.

"RICE!" says Emily.

"Okay," answers Rhondi. "I'm glad you're thinking, but Rest, Ice, Compression, and Elevation won't work here. That's for sprains."

"Direct pressure to stop the bleeding?" asks Ayisha.

"Very good!" says Rhondi. She motions me over and tilts my chin up with her thumb. I stifle my sniffles. "There's just a little cut on your lip there, Molly. And some swelling. Push on it with your thumb." She drops her hand. "You think you can keep going or do you want to sit on the curb for a few minutes?"

I stop pressing my lip with my thumb and wrap my arms around my blistered, bleeding, sunburned self. "I want to go home."

"You're going to quit?" The Great Caped one leans close to me. Oh Lord. Please, let this not herald a motivational speech. She quiets her voice. "Molly, *please*. It's not good for the girls to see you quit over a scrape."

I try to clarify and whisper back. "I just didn't know I'd be walking so much today."

"Well, it is a *walk*athon."

"My feet hurt. And now my lip."

"All you have to do is put one foot in front of the other. We don't have that much longer to go." She stretches out her arms and rests them on my shoulders. I wince.

"Sunburn," I squeak.

"Sorry." She drops her hands onto her hips. "Go at your own pace. You can do it, Molly."

"I want to go home," I repeat.

Rhondi's lips purse; I think she's starting to get angry, which reminds me that for a moment there, she was actually being kind of nice. "You said you were committed. This is not some leisurely stroll you can opt out of. This is a walk for muscular dystrophy." Her voice lowers a decibel. "Think of the message you'll be sending to these girls if you quit. Especially over a little bump on your lip? Where is your sense of follow-through? Emily alone raised three hundred dollars."

I glance over at them, this flock of little girls with red capes and smiles oozing with optimism, eyebrows raised in hope. Rhondi continues, her voice louder now. "In the Corps, we follow through with what we say we're going to do."

"What about my shoe?" I lift up my mangled flip-flop.

"One of our core values is resourcefulness." She pulls a small first-aid box from her backpack and opens its lid. "What do you think, girls?"

A few minutes later, my flip-flop has been bound to my foot with surgical tape, thanks to Maribel. Then, like a drill sergeant, Rhondi turns to the girls, who are now in a single-file line, and booms, "One foot in front of the other, girls!" We start walking behind her. I hold up the end of the line.

Rhondi falls back and gives me a nod. "See? You might be stronger than you think." She picks up speed and resumes her space in front of the line. "Who are we?" Rhondi shouts.

"Girl Corps!" the girls shout back.

"And what's at our core?" Rhondi asks.

"Connection! Opinion! Resourcefulness! Enlightenment!"

I'm stronger than I think. I repeat that phrase in my mind. I tread along on my sore feet with my split lip and look up to the sky for a sign of hope. All I see are clouds, so I cast my eyes down and watch as I put one foot in front of the other.

By the time the whole thing is over and we approach the park from the gravelly lot, my right foot has lost circulation. "We did it!" shouts Hatsuku, her cheeks puffed up with pride.

"Yay!" a few others shout.

"Yes!" I yell. My enthusiasm is real. I just completed a twelve-mile walk. I didn't raise any money, personally, but it's good deed by association.

"Look, you guys, food!" shouts Maribel, and we rush toward the picnic table in the distance where Dede now stands. The girls follow me and we actually dare to pass Rhondi, who doesn't seem to mind too much as we hurry ahead.

Even after I down a sixteen-ounce electric-blue sports drink, the hole in my stomach doesn't feel filled, so I reach for a crustless heart-shaped sandwich, then cram it down.

Three peanut butter and honey sandwiches later, a glob of wet concrete has formed at the bottom of my stomach, which clogs the sense of accomplishment I felt ten minutes ago.

"Circle time, girls!" Rhondi waves at the girls to come to her. Sophia rebels and scuffs along behind the group. I wait by the picnic table, where only crumbs are left scattered across the food platters. These girls can pound down the chow.

"Molly?" Rhondi calls. "You too. Come join us."

There's a flicker of electricity inside me as the group beckons me. When I reach them, we attempt to create a circle, but each girl—except for Sophia, who stands with her arms crossed next to Rhondi—vies for a position next to me.

"I want to stand by Molly!" shouts Maribel.

"No! She came with me," says Claire.

"But I was here first!" yells Ayisha, with a death grip on my hand.

"Whoa, girls," I say, "no need to argue. I'll just—"

"Girls!" Rhondi interrupts. "Control yourselves." Ayisha keeps hold of my right hand and Claire clings to my left one. The blob of us becomes more of a circle, our fingers intertwined.

"I'm proud of you." Rhondi makes an effort to look each one of us in the eyes, and I don't resist when she fixes her eyes on mine. "You finished the course and raised seven hundred and fifty-seven dollars for muscular dystrophy. Let's hear your voices sing!"

As the girls raise their hands, mine go up as well.

I don't know the song, but I wave my arms with theirs.

> *"Connecting to each other, our opinions voiced so clear,*
> *Resourceful and enlightened, for we need never fear!*
> *Learning, growing, changing on each journey that we*
>   *chart,*
> *A girl to the core today, forever a girl at heart!"*

I wish they'd sing it again so I could become more familiar with the words. Except the girls whoop and holler, which suddenly gives me an eerie feeling that this is not unlike how I envision cheerleading camp. It's actually sort of a cult, the girls surrounding me as caped, uniformed clones.

But they're not clones. I got to see their individual personalities today and actually enjoyed them. I'm even grateful they distracted me from a day that might have otherwise been filled with soggy Kleenexes, blow-torched photographs of Trevor, and excessive self-pity.

"See, Molly?" says Ayisha, still holding my hand. "You did it."

"Of course she did it," says Claire, as if she knew all along that I could. I guess that's saying more than I thought of myself, and I give her hand a gentle squeeze.

Dede steps over to us. "We should get going. Grandma and Dad are waiting for us, Claire."

I turn to Ayisha. "It was nice meeting you."

"Aren't you coming back?"

"Oh, I don't think so." I want to, though. Is that as crazy as it sounds? "But I live right next door to Claire. You can come by and say hi with her next time you two play, okay?"

Ayisha gives me a warm hug, alerting the other girls to my departure.

"You're leaving?" says Maribel.

"Yep, but you did great today." I reach down and give one of her ponytails a playful tug.

"I hope your lip's okay," says Emily.

"I'll be fine. From what you said about your braces, I guess it could have been worse." She nods in agreement.

From the picnic table, Rhondi says, "Girls, we still have some business to tend to over here. Come on."

They start toward Rhondi, turning back to wave.

"Bye, everyone," I say.

"Bye, Molly!" the girls yell. I wave but keep moving on aching feet.

Dede unlocks the car via remote and I lunge for the backseat before I'm assigned shotgun. Once I sit down, my body collapses.

"Wasn't that fun?" Claire asks excitedly. I don't know where this girl gets her energy. "Twelve miles! We walked twelve miles!"

"It's wonderful, Claire."

"Mom? Will you put on *Phantom*?"

Dede and Claire spend the drive home singing tunes from *The Phantom of the Opera*, which I highly doubt Andrew Lloyd Webber intended to be sung in the key of screechy cat.

I check my phone, where ten text messages from Vanessa can be summed up by one: SLEAZEBALL TREVOR!

The afterglow of the walk starts to fade and I begin to play dead. I'm going home now to my real life, where I'm not Molly at the walkathon but Molly with the cheating boyfriend. Molly who has to figure out how she's going to face him at school. It was easier just to walk than to have to think about my life.

I tilt my head toward the air-conditioning vent above me. It feels good against the sting of sunburn on my face.

When Dede drops me off in front of my house, I step back out into the heat in my tape-footed sandal and hobble toward my front door. "Thanks," I say.

"Oh, Molly." Dede looks at me with gratitude. "Thank *you*."

"Thanks, Molly!" shouts Claire.

Granddad has written me a note in his chicken-scratch cursive and left it on the entry table.

> *At the Banshee. Karaoke tonight! Call me if you'd like me to come get you. Not sure when the others will be home from work.*

In the kitchen, I use Uncle Murph's favorite paring knife to remove the tape and grubby flip-flop from my hoof. Once it's off, my street-blackened foot becomes free, a bony bird released from a cruel cage.

Upstairs in my attic room, I hop in the shower, where I let cold water trickle over my burned shoulders, my red arms, my cut calf, and my blistered, gashed-up feet.

What was the tune of that Girl Corps song again? It started low, then crept up high. I close my eyes, the water falling over my face. I pretend I'm holding Buttons, arranging my fingers where I think the song would land. And it comes to me.

Connecting to each other, la, la, la, la, de da—
Resourceful and enlightened, for we need never fear!

I tap out as much as I can remember. The coolness from the shower continues to feel good against the heat of my skin.

After I'm out, I remove my contacts, spread aloe lotion all over my body, and crawl into bed with wet, tangled hair. Sleep should hammer me over the head, but instead, I'm brought back to where I was this morning before I crawled out from underneath the covers: Trevor. I grab the smooth wooden sculpture of Mom and hold it close to me, curling myself into a ball.

Tears seep into my pillow, until it feels like my head is resting on a gigantic tea bag. My mind trails back to the walkathon, the faces of the girls. A giggle escapes. So weird to be there today. And I felt something when I left. Accomplishment. Just like Rhondi said: "We are what we do." If that's true, we are what we don't do, either. That's got to mean something, too.

. . .

The muted pounding of a fist at the front door wakes me. It's still light outside. My sheets stick to me like I'm a sausage wrapped in cabbage leaves—a favorite menu item at the Banshee. My lip throbs with pain. I may have slept five minutes or an entire twenty-four hours, I don't know. It's dusky, I can tell that much.

The clock reads 5:36 p.m. I've only slept a few hours.

The thudding on the door gets more persistent. I stumble out of bed, look out my window, and see Vanessa's little blue tin-can car parked next to the curb. I'm glad she's here, but for some reason, I'd rather be back in the arms of peaceful sleep.

With my glasses on, I take a quick look in the mirror. My upper lip has doubled in size; my red face gives the impression that I'm holding my breath. I officially look as crappy on the outside as I feel on the inside.

Downstairs, I open the front door and Vanessa bursts in like the Amazon woman she is, her dark brown hair loose over her broad shoulders. Her low-slung jeans reveal what's just above her waistline and what's just below her belly button.

She flings her purse on the floor in the entry hall, at the base of the Virgin Mary portrait, Mary's arms open wide as if she's been waiting for an oversized brown faux-leather purse all these years.

"I'm so sorry, Molly." Nessa scans me, head to toe. "It's that bad, huh?" She leans into me. "Kissies." We peck each other's cheeks and I smell the stale aftereffect of a cigarette. Blech. She started smoking last year, and it's a habit I can't seem to talk her out of.

She pulls away, surveying my face again. "Man, you are beet red. And what happened to your lip? Looks like you got a triple shot of collagen."

"Shut up. I fell."

"Fell where?" She peers at me. "You're not trying to cover anything up, are you? Did he *hit* you?"

"No! Seriously, I fell face-first on the sidewalk doing a walkathon."

She winces. "That had to hurt." She pulls back; her black-eyelinered eyes squinch. "Wait, what were you doing at a walkathon?"

"I did it for Claire and those Girl Corps girls. They raised close to a thousand bucks. We walked twelve miles."

"Good deeds, Mol. You're always doing the right thing. I just hope you've already forgotten about that poohead Trevor."

My shoulders slump. "Not exactly."

"Come on." Vanessa leads me through the hallway and into the den, where she plops into Uncle Murph's brown La-Z-Boy and I fall into Uncle Garrett's beige one.

I touch my puffy lip and wonder for a second how Trevor's ear is holding up.

"You know"—she swivels in the chair—"this is actually good timing to break it off with Trevor, because I happen to have something that I'm pretty sure will make you feel better." She launches out of the La-Z-Boy and runs to the hallway, coming back with her purse.

I could have saved myself a lot of crying if I'd known that the answer to my problems was inside Vanessa's purse. She extracts four boxes of Junior Mints and shakes them like they're noisemakers. "For you."

"Thanks." She knows these are my favorite. And at the Buck Stops Here, where she works, you can get four boxes of chocolate-covered anythings for a dollar. I pry open the cardboard and shake a warm, melted lump of Junior Mints directly into my mouth. The delicious mint tingles along my tongue.

"Now to the big score." Her hand disappears back into her purse and reappears with her wallet, from which she tugs out a square of scratch paper with a phone number.

"What's that?"

"This, Mol, is our plan for tonight."

"You're kidding, right? I don't want to go anywhere. I'm thinking we stay in."

"Now, hold on. You might change your mind." She hunches down in her storyteller mode. "So, I'm in aisle seven today at work, the one with all the tools and car stuff?"

"Yeah?"

"I was hanging packages of those air fresheners that dangle from the rearview. And this guy grabs a pine tree one from right over my shoulder and tells me pine reminds him of the mountains."

"That's deep, Nessa."

"I know, it's not revelatory. But Mol, I look over my shoulder at him and it's Karl."

She waits for my reaction, but I don't know who she's talking about. "Karl?"

"Karl!" she squeaks. "Drummer of Razor Hurley."

"Oh, yeah." Razor Hurley is the little alternative rock band that can't. They have one bootleg album: *Hell's Butterfly*. Nessa knows all the lyrics by heart; I know them by default, the worst song being "Acorns and Whiskey."

"Well," she says, playfully flipping her mane of brown hair. "They're playing at the Poseidon tonight. And I have a personal invite from Karl—hot drummer—to get a sneak peek backstage." She screams in glee. "We're going to see Razor Hurley tonight, Mol!"

I finger the edge of my empty Junior Mints box. "Ness, I don't want to go."

"Seriously? Do you know what you're refusing here? We're talking backstage with one of our favorite bands."

One of *her* favorite bands, actually.

She reaches her foot out to tickle the bottom of my own. "Look, I know you're hurt, okay? But it's not the end of the world. This whole thing with Trevor? It's a blessing, when you think about it. We're too young to be tied down."

Like mother, like daughter. Vanessa's mom is a chronic dater. Each weekend she's out with *someone*, doing a mysterious *something*. "I thought he was the *one*, Ness."

"There's a better *one* out there for you." She points at me. "The sooner you pick yourself up, the easier it's going to be to get over him. You can stay home and mope or you can do like you did this morning with that walk and get out in the world and kick its ass."

The Girl Corps walk did take my mind off things, but I know that going out tonight is not going to make me feel better. "Okay, but a walk for charity is different than going to a bar to see Razor Hurley."

"It may *look* different, but it's about getting out and moving on." For a second Vanessa sounds like Rhondi with her *one foot in front of the other* motto.

"The Poseidon is twenty-one and over. Plus, isn't it, like, located in an alley where some dude was murdered last year?"

"Yeah." She wipes the fact away with her hand as if it's a bothersome little fly of a detail. "That was a whole drug-related thing."

I give her my patented "Seriously?" look.

"Stop worrying. We're gonna be inside the place. Karl told me exactly what to do. There's a back door, a secret knock—" She bends down and raps the coffee table with her gypsy-looking hands, three fingers on each hand circled by silver: *rat, rat, tat-tat-tat, rat*.

"I'm glad you've got the whole secret-clubhouse-knock thing going with Karl, but I'm not up for it." I throw my head back against the headrest of the recliner. "Just go without me. Or call Jasmine or something." Jasmine's a year older than we are and more of a gossip hound—very different from me. Thankfully, Vanessa manages to keep Jasmine and me filed in separate compartments of her life.

Vanessa scrapes a finger against the soft weave of fabric along the La-Z-Boy armrest. "What's it gonna take, Molly? We've hardly hung out since you and Trevor have been together. I'm not complaining about it, okay? I just think we could use a night out together."

She vaults out of her chair. "I'm covering Bo's eight-hour shift tomorrow, so it's not like we're going to be home really late, anyway." Bo is Nessa's coworker and a senior at Hilldale who has an extraordinary amount of facial hair. "So do it for me?"

I feel like I'm slipping now. Whereas before I was holding firm to what I wanted, this whole do-it-for-me thing has me losing my grip. I *have* been a terrible friend. Nessa sent me text messages all day long, trying to cheer me up. Even brought me Junior Mints. And it's true, I've spent hardly any time with her.

"Fine," I answer.

"Yes!" Nessa flies up onto the coffee table, her arms shoot up, and she shakes her hips.

"Okay, but no guys. And if we get there and there's security or people look at us like they know we're too young, you have to promise me that we won't go in."

With her palm in swear position she says, "Promise. And you will not be sorry. You need this. Trust me."

I look into her black-brown eyes. Eyes that I've always managed to trust. Granddad used to tell me about his childhood cottage in Ireland, where the waters outside his door were filled with seals. He would sometimes sneak out of his bed at night, hoping to find a selkie, a dark creature that would shed her rubbery seal skin at night and transform into a beautiful, alluring dark-haired, dark-eyed woman who'd be impossible to resist. He never saw one, although he dreamed of many.

On numerous occasions I've wondered if Nessa might be one of those creatures, because she has a way of pulling me in that I can't exactly explain. I think when I was younger, I'd go along with her because of that glint in her eye that symbolized her get-up-and-go attitude. It's the same sparkle in her that makes me curious enough to see where she's going to take me, except I'm starting to think that curiosity might be a lack of my own imagination, the absence of my own sense of mystery.

There's no way to describe what it smells like backstage at the Poseidon other than a mingling of cigarette smoke and man sweat: an aroma that I highly recommend *not* become a candle scent. Sure, the stage here is large enough to have this backstage area, but still, it's no bigger than a walk-in closet.

Razor Hurley has just finished its first ear-stabbing set, and the shaggy, string-bean-shaped bass player stands next to me, nursing a big bottle of Jack Daniel's. "Cool," he says, pulling the word spontaneously out of the air.

"Excuse me?" I ask.

He turns. His long hair veils what might be his face. "We can hook up, 'cause you look good."

I now further regret wearing the clothes Vanessa lent me when she picked me up tonight: low-cut black blouse, tight jeans, and leather wedge sandals that currently strangle my already sore feet.

"What do you say?" he asks. I jump back and run to the dark corner where Vanessa and drummer Karl, who is also of the string-bean physique, are making out. Their mouths smack together as Karl's hands get lost in the thick of her hair.

I want to get out of here. *"Nessa?"* She turns her head slightly, because I guess it's too inconvenient for her to stop kissing Karl. She opens an eye and shakes her head.

"C'mon, Ness," I beg. "I want to go home."

She reaches her hand out to me, her finger wagging no.

"You *promised*," I say, more forcefully. This is awful and uncomfortable. Bass boy scuffs back over to me. Nessa wags her finger again, which makes me suddenly want to grab it and bite it off.

I hate when she gets like this, immovable. She was like this earlier, too, when I didn't want to come here, but I surrendered because of my stupid guilt about being a bad friend. I mean, if *she* were a good friend, she would have realized that I'm hurting right now and could have used a night in with a bowl of popcorn and a sappy movie.

The Jack Daniel's bottle appears in front of my face like a torch, an offering from the bass player. "You want?"

"No." I need to get out of here, but if I go back

outside, I might get murdered by some crystal meth junkie.

There's a black shower curtain barrier between "backstage" and the bar itself. I peek out to see if it's safe to enter. I'm not sure what would happen if I got caught in the bar—Aunt Tip and Clem have kicked out maybe a handful of people who tried using fake IDs to order a drink—but I'm not going to order. All I want is freedom from the Jack Daniel's minion.

Behind me, I can feel his hand on my waist. "Nice," he says. With that, I walk out onto the other side of the shower curtain. It's crowded in the bar, but I spot a small table in the corner. There's no chair, but it's dark enough that I can blend in with the scenery, so I hurry toward it.

I'll just lie low until the band goes back onstage, and then I'll drag Vanessa out of here. Good luck to me. I could always call the Banshee for someone to come and get me. It's the worst-case scenario, but I'm not ruling it out. I'd rather have Daddy come get me alive than dead in the alley.

The Poseidon is much more savage than what I'm used to at the Banshee. The walls are painted black except for a mural behind the bar, depicting a huge man with rippling muscles holding a spear that actually looks more like a dinner fork. Thank you, freshman English, for the Greek mythology unit last year, because I recognize the man as Poseidon, god of the sea. Ms. Pinkwater might appreciate the fact that I recognize the medium as oil paint, but then again, that has nothing to do with ceramics.

I stand at my empty table, which has a wood surface not much bigger than a dinner plate. I'm definitely more exposed out here, even behind my tiny table, so I keep my eyes cast down, hoping my ballooned lip and barbecued face won't draw attention.

Engravings cover the plywood surface of the table, which reveals that bars aren't really that different from high school classrooms. I scrape my nail into the peeled wood. *T* for Trevor.

A week ago tonight, Trevor and I were eating pizza and playing footsie under a table, which was bigger than this sorry excuse for a surface. We went back to his house and watched a horror flick, *Ditto Man,* about a guy who repairs copy machines by day and morphs into a serial killer at night, preying upon the innocent secretaries he has met in the offices he's serviced. The movie sucked, but I enjoyed nuzzling closer to Trevor each time the killer approached his shrieking victims. I wish I were back where I was last week, with pizza, *Ditto Man,* and the freshly showered scent of Trevor, ignorant of what was to come.

The one thing about the walkathon today is that it was planned. There was a route we followed. If I had stayed home I might have given in and called Trevor, but the walk kept me focused. If I don't have a plan, I might give in when I see Trevor at school on Monday, face to face on campus or within the hot, muggy walls of ceramics class.

"What can I get you?" I look up and there's a waitress in red short-shorts with a tray perched on her hip, a Bic pen held between her fingers, ready to take an order.

Poop-crap! "Oh, uh, no thanks." I pull back my vandalizing hand.

She rolls her eyes at me. "The tables are used to set *drinks* on. You can't stand here if you're not going to order."

I keep my head tilted down. "I'm—I'm so sorry. I'll move."

"Wait—" She stops me by placing her free hand on my shoulder. I grit my teeth at the contact she's made with my sunburn, then manage to look back at her, my head still strained downward. She narrows her eyes at me. "Can I see your ID?"

Think. Think! "I'm not thirsty. Thanks. I'll just move."

"I didn't *ask* if you were thirsty. I asked for your ID."

Cries of joy trail through the bar as the band mounts the small stage. The electric-guitar guy slices through some slurry chords. Uncle Rourke would blow him out of the water with his own Fender. The singer chimes in, screaming as if he's being electrocuted.

"Really," I tell the waitress. "I'll just leave. I don't have—"

Vanessa approaches. "What's going on here?" If she were close enough, I'd kick her under the table—if there were a big enough table to kick under. Instead, I shake my head briskly so she'll just shut up.

Vanessa scowls at the waitress. "We showed our IDs at the door," she lies. "Plus, we're with the guys in the band. In fact, we were even backstage with them."

The waitress fails to be impressed. "I don't care if you were backstage with the Dalai Lama." She taps her pen on the tray next to a discarded maraschino cherry stem, then holds out her hand toward Vanessa. "I need to see some identification."

"I've got nothing to hide." Vanessa changes her tactic, and cool as any refrigerated cucumber, she slides an ID from her pocket, holds it between her pointer and middle fingers, and passes it over to the waitress, who scrutinizes it.

She has a fake ID? I can't believe she would bring me into battle knowing I don't have a weapon! "Come with me," says the waitress, still in possession of Vanessa's ID.

I follow, but Vanessa grabs my hand. "We're not going anywhere with you," she says, and pulls me back. The waitress turns to look at us.

I lean closer to Vanessa and whisper, "Stop it, Ness."

Naturally, she doesn't listen.

"You have no right to take away my ID!" Vanessa screams over the music.

The waitress ignores her and slips through the crowd on the dance floor. "You think you could stop making a scene, Vanessa? They're gonna call the cops. Stop it, okay?"

We watch the waitress snake over to the bouncer at the entrance. Nessa says, "You're the one who came out here into plain view, Molly. Now I have to do damage control. I only came out here to find *you*. You should have stayed backstage."

I glare at her overly made-up face. "Right, Vanessa. I should've stayed backstage and let the bass player have his way with me." I shake my head and clench my teeth. The waitress winds back toward us, Buff Bouncer following. "Oh God! We're definitely busted."

Nessa says, "What are you worried about, anyway? We're not gonna get in trouble. When in your life has your dad ever punished you?"

"It's not about getting in trouble, Nessa. It's about letting him down. Which I doubt you could understand."

"Don't tell me I don't understand," she hisses. "Here they come. Just let me do the talking."

Buff Bouncer, dressed in all black from the tip of his button-up shirt collar to the heel of his butt-kicking military boots, arrives with the short-shorts waitress, who stands behind him, happy as a little clam.

The polyester fabric of the shirt I borrowed from Nessa clings tighter to my skin as sweat starts to percolate from the well of my pores.

He holds Nessa's ID in his outstretched palm. "This is good."

Vanessa flicks her long hair back and as she reaches out for her ID, she smirks at the waitress. "I told you."

Buff Bouncer's hand quickly retreats. "But the hologram is crap."

"I don't have an ID," I confess. "I'm sorry. We'll leave." The waitress smiles her pearly whitened teeth in victory.

"What are you talking about?" says Nessa, looking at me as if my truth were a lie. She points to the ID in Buff Bouncer's hand. "That's my driver's license. I need it. Hand it over before I have to contact the authorities."

"Nessa," I say under my breath.

Buff Bouncer laughs. "The *authorities*?" His face goes straight. "*I'm* the authority, and I'm telling both of you to come with me."

Nessa clutches my wrist like a too-tight handcuff. "Never mind. We're leaving." I wriggle my arm free.

"No you don't," he says, barring her path with his steely arm.

Nessa steps forward, but now I grab her arm. She eyes me with surprise. She's not used to me fighting back. I'm not used to it, either, but she's out of control. I guess I've forgotten how stubborn and wild she can be. It's not even wild as much as it is stupid.

We follow Buff Bouncer past the bar and down the hall, where we're paraded past the massive line that has formed outside the ladies' room. He keeps close to Vanessa, as if she might bolt.

Buff leads us to a door at the end of the hall. A red

and gold placard reads: MANAGER. We slow our pace. Nessa leans in to me. "Stay calm, Molly, or you're gonna make us look like fools."

"Me?" I can't believe her. "You don't think you already covered that territory?"

"Just shut up and let me do the talking."

"It's your *talking* that got me into this in the first place."

"Don't blame me, Molly," she lashes back. "You're a big girl."

She's right about that. I was dumb enough to listen to her. It's my fault. Daddy's going to have to find out about this, because something's gonna happen, cops or no cops.

It's not that I'm going to get in trouble. Nessa was right about that. I've only seen Daddy lose his temper once, several years back, when he screamed bloody murder and hurled his boot into the garage window after he stepped on a three-inch nail. It's not the anger in him that scares me, anyway. It's the quiet in him, the wordless disappointment I see sometimes when he loses a bid on a job.

I've just got to tell the truth, because unlike Nessa, I have no desire to make this worse for us.

The cheap hollow door to the manager's office hardly makes a sound after Buff knocks and then opens it to reveal a small man wearing a black blazer with a white T-shirt underneath. He sits behind a desk and looks like he's slathered himself in baby oil. His long dark hair is slicked back like he's either a bail bondsman or an offspring of the Godfather.

He nods to Buff Bouncer, who tells him, "We got two fakers here."

Greasy Manager Man replies, "C'mon in."

We click our high-heel-sandaled feet into the office—I feel even more stupid now, like we're really playing dress-up and we don't belong. The walls of the office are covered with frayed-at-the-edges posters of women in G-strings holding beer bottles and leaning on shiny black cars. I'm now scared *and* disgusted.

"Sit," Greasy Manager Man says.

Immediately, I seat myself in one of two worn tweed chairs facing his desk.

Vanessa refuses. "I'll stand."

Greasy Manager Man's eyes linger on Vanessa and her well-endowed parts. "I'm calling your parents or the cops. You choose." Nessa's mom is in Vegas this weekend. There's no other option but my family unit.

Hell-ass-damn! Maybe Daddy *will* get angry about this. I don't know what that looks like. But I'd much rather have him find out about this from me than from the police, *that* much I know.

Nessa starts to say something, but, fed up, I blurt out the number of the only place that I know can save us.

When I called the Banshee, Daddy and the uncles weren't there just yet. I'm not saying Daddy won't find out, but I'm relieved it's Granddad who's coming to get us. At least Granddad will take Vanessa home, so when I see Daddy, I can explain what happened without her jumping into a lie that I won't be able to defend.

Nessa and I sit on the ground outside the entrance in our dictated time-out spots on either side of Buff Bouncer, who sits above us on his steel stool, playing gatekeeper and checking the IDs of the people waiting in line to get into the Poseidon.

I keep watch on the parking lot for Granddad's shiny black GTO, which I would have expected to show up right away since we're a five-minute drive from the Banshee. Maybe he hit all the traffic lights, because we've been waiting more than fifteen minutes for his arrival.

Nessa picks at a scab on her knee. I'm so pissed off at her right now. The entire time we've been sitting out here I've gone through different conversations in my head. From "Why didn't you tell me you had a fake ID?" to "I can't believe you didn't shut up in there and just let us walk out."

The Girl Corps founders, Frances and Lila Larson, had to fight to be listened to. I remember that from what I read to Claire last night. They had to stop picking fallen apples from the dirt and demand higher ground, but it's hard to stand your ground against someone who doesn't listen. "I didn't want to come here, Nessa. Didn't you hear me say that?"

She peels the edge of her scab. "Yes, I heard you say that. You wanted to be sad and depressed at home and I, being your friend, wanted to get you out."

"Yeah?" Now I've got her. She's no longer preoccupied with her scab, and she looks me in the eye.

"You never listen to me," I say.

She rests her chin on her knuckles. "I'm sorry, okay? It's just hard for me to see you upset. It didn't make sense that you'd sit at home when we could be having fun here."

"Fun?"

She smiles. "Okay, maybe this isn't the way I pictured our night together, but you can't deny that it was an adventure. You only live once, right?"

"Tonight was a fiasco, Ness. Not an adventure."

"Well, that's what makes us different. I don't see it

the way you do. We're not the same, but that's a good thing. We balance each other out."

Maybe that's how it used to be, but it's downright annoying when her part of the scale gets more airtime than mine. It's not even about airtime, either. It's about feeling like my voice isn't valid.

A loud engine roars into the parking lot and I see Aunt Tipper's silver 1981 Lincoln Town Car. Aunt Tip sits in the driver's seat, where I can see the straps of her apron. Daddy sits shotgun, his face pinched.

I may have underestimated his reaction to all this. My heart stops, my stomach sinks—all the shutdown stuff that happens when one is in a state of utter terror. I've got to face him here and now with this. Tell him I'm sorry, it won't happen again. That I was being stupid. That it's not a reflection on him.

"That's our ride," Vanessa says to Buff Bouncer. I stand up next to her. She whispers, "I thought your grandpa was coming." Her confusion is about one thousand times more subdued than the strong urge I have to fling myself in the front of a diesel truck and call it a day.

Aunt Tip's Town Car dips into a pothole and rises back up, the huge hood of the car aimed at us.

I look at Daddy, whose face is still hardened, and now that he's closer, I see that it's red, too. It's the kind of expression he has when he's pulled the cord on the lawn mower ten times but it still won't start. This *is* worse than I thought.

Aunt Tipper's window is rolled down because, as always, when Aunt Tip is outside the jurisdiction of California's smoking laws, she's got a lit ready-to-puff Virginia Slims nearby.

Right now, said cigarette is being sucked for all it's worth.

"Girls!" she yells. "Get in the car." A plume of smoke rushes out the side of her mouth.

She and Buff Bouncer exchange a few words at the car window while Vanessa and I scurry into the immaculate red plush backseat of the smoke-filled car.

Daddy rears his head at us. "What the *hell* are you doing here?"

"It's my fault," Vanessa asserts. She shoulders the blame that earlier she said was mine.

"Wow," Daddy says, with feigned awe. "What a friend. I do think Molly had something to do with you being here, no?"

"I'm not denying it," I say. "I just wasn't thinking."

"You're damn right you weren't thinking!" Daddy yells. "And that there—" He leans over, peers at my lip. "Someone in there hit you?" His nostrils flare. It's the closest I've ever seen him to rage.

"No, I fell on that walk today."

He closes his eyes for a second. "Good." Good that I fell or good that I wasn't hit?

Buff Bouncer finishes talking with Aunt Tip and walks back over to his stool. She turns and points at us with two fingers, her Virginia Slims locked between them. "You two should consider yourselves lucky. This is no place for two birds like you, unless you're aiming to be a pair of slappers. And in that case, I'd say you got yourselves in the right establishment." I should have listened to myself.

"Let's go, Tip," Daddy says as he turns around to face the windshield. "I'm so disappointed in you, Molly!" He slams his hand on the dashboard, the action itself showing how understated his words are. I don't know how to un-disappoint someone.

Aunt Tip puffs her cigarette and gives us a good stare, then exhales. "Have some respect for yourselves. I swear, if your necklines dipped any lower, I'd be able to see your knobs." I look down at the line of cleavage that intersects the scoop of the black shirt.

Disgusted, she shifts out of park and drives. I turn to look at Vanessa, whose shirt is even lower than mine. She widens her eyes at me. "Excuse me?" Vanessa says. Oh Jesus, Mary, and Joseph! Will she ever stop?

Aunt Tip slams on the brakes, which causes Nessa to reel back. "What?"

Vanessa leans forward again. "It's just that I drove here. I don't want to leave my car. It's parked on the street."

Daddy shakes his head. "You let that be the least of your worries. You can walk yourself over here tomorrow to get your car, but tonight, we're taking you home."

Vanessa retreats and eases back in the seat, finally quiet.

The cabin of the car remains silent after we drop Vanessa off at her apartment complex and head toward the Banshee.

When we enter the pub, Daddy and I ignore the mass salutations as Aunt Tipper resumes her place behind the bar. I follow Daddy across the parquet dance floor, down the back hallway, and into Aunt Tip's office. Granddad and the uncles acknowledge me from the booth in the back of the restaurant, but it's a quiet kind of hello. No shouts. No "Molly B!"

Saturday is karaoke night, so there's the horrible sound of a man belting out "Country roads! Take me home . . . to the place . . . I belong!" A popular pick among fiftysomethings. John Denver is no doubt rolling in his grave.

Inside Aunt Tip's windowless office Daddy motions to the plaid couch and commands, "Sit down." The faint squeak of the John Denver man's voice seeps under the door. Daddy paces from one side of the room to the other.

"That was really stupid of you going into that place tonight, Molly. You know that?"

"It was stupid." I nod quickly.

He stops pacing and sits at the edge of Aunt Tip's massive oak desk. He raps it a few times with his knuckles, his straight hair falling down over his eyes. I don't know what he's going to say, and the unsaid makes me cower on the couch.

He tips his head back. "You know, you were

practically raised at the Banshee, so I'm not gonna say that you being around drunk gee-eyed fellas most of your life hasn't affected you." He scratches his nose with his thumb, slow to continue. "And I know you not having your mam around can't be easy. God knows not one of us is a saint substitute for an angel like her."

His hand makes a fist again and knocks on the desk, punctuating his words. "But in no way did any of us— your granddad, uncles, your auntie—ever think we were raising you to think life is about getting fluthered and hanging around seedy places. If that's what you've gotten from this family after all these years, we've done you wrong."

I bite the inside of my cheek and try to keep the tremor out of my windpipe. "That's not it, Daddy. Not at all." The Banshee has always been a symbol of good food, music, and people coming together, albeit as the evening wears on, sometimes drunk, uncoordinated people coming together. "I know I shouldn't have gone into that place with Vanessa."

He gestures toward me, but the words don't come out right away. "You—you act like you just followed her in there. Did I raise you to jump off a bridge if someone asked you? Are you that *mindless*, Molly?"

"You don't understand. It's more complicated than that. There's a lot going on, and Nessa figured me going with her would cheer me up and take my mind off things. I didn't want to go, except I didn't listen to myself." I look down at my knees in shame. "I don't do that very well."

"Look," Daddy says, peering at me. "We all make mistakes and fooster around in the wrong places sometimes, but you, you got a good head on your shoulders." He sighs heavily. "I don't understand why you wouldn't trust yourself. Is it something I've done to make you think that you can't trust yourself, Molly? Is it?"

"No, it's not you." I try to help him out. "I've got a lot of stuff going on right now is all. Stuff that I've never dealt with before."

"What stuff, girl?" he asks with desperation in his voice. " 'Stuff' doesn't tell me anything."

I gaze down at my lap. "Trevor stuff. He lied about something. We broke up."

"That's what's bothering you?"

"Yeah."

He sits next to me on the couch. "We do stupid things when we're hurt. But let me save you some grief. When you feel bad, it's often best to do nothing at all. Remember that it's no delay to stop and edge the tool, because if you rush into something you haven't thought through, you'll regret it."

He holds my hand in his, carefully, like it's a delicate seashell. "You have to work things out for yourself, but that doesn't mean you go looking for trouble. You keep your head about you."

I look down at my hand wrapped up in Daddy's

calloused one. Keep my head about me? I don't even know where to start. I think that's how I got myself into this mess. "I don't know who I am, Daddy."

"Hey." He lifts my chin. "It's never too late to find out."

I wake at five-thirty on Sunday morning in a cold sweat, having dreamed I gave birth to Trevor during PE. One minute I was huffing around the dirt track, the next I was on my back next to the drinking fountain, my royal blue nylon PE shorts pulled down to my knees, giving birth to a full-sized and hairless naked Trevor who looked as if he were covered in a jar of Ragú spaghetti sauce. Ick.

I sit up in bed, my legs heavy with soreness. I reach and touch my mother, set the statue on my knee, and trace the tiny nub of her nose. It would have been nice if she had been buried instead of cremated after her funeral. Then I could take her flowers and rub her tombstone clean with my sleeve. But what's left of her physically was flown back to Ireland and sprinkled in the ocean off Mama's favorite place, the Dingle

Peninsula, which on a map looks like the claw of a bear's paw. Sometimes I go on the Internet and look at images of it. It gives me calm, knowing Mom is somewhere beautiful. Somewhere I'll be able to visit one day.

Nessa and I texted back and forth a little late last night.

Nessa: U IN TRBLE?

Me: DAD MAD. NO MORE POSEIDON ADVENTURE, NESS.

Nessa: K. I PIC U UP MON MORN.

I'm going to have to stop my tagalong with Nessa, but we've been friends for so long, I can't cut her out of my life like she's a mole that needs to be removed. Maybe we can work this out. Maybe the stronger I get, the more she'll listen. At least I talked back to her last night. A little.

I can smell the strong nutty scent of coffee once I walk downstairs, past the closed doors of Daddy's and Uncle Rourke's rooms. Granddad sits at the round kitchen table, his blue shirt buttoned up all the way to his neck, his wooly hair somewhat tame. How someone can look so fresh this early in the morning is beyond me. The Sunday paper is sprawled before him like a tablecloth.

"Well, you're up early, Molly B. You're two for two. No more sleeping in on the weekend?"

I take a seat next to him, fold my arms on the table, and rest my head. "I'm just having trouble sleeping."

He looks down at his paper casually. "That's a surprise. Your aunt Tip got back to the Banshee after bringing you and your da home last night. She told me that you and your lass Vanessa were twisting the hay a bit."

"Yeah, well, you don't need to worry about me. I won't be doing that again."

He turns the page of his newspaper. "I'm not worried about you, Molly."

I sit up. "You're not?"

He looks over the edge of the paper. "Nah. I've seen some scrubbers in my life, and you're not one of 'em." His confidence in me feels good.

"Thanks, Granddad."

"So"—he keeps his head buried in the paper—"there was a bag with your name on it on the porch next to my newspaper this morning. I set it on the hall table."

I jump out of my chair, banging into its edge. The coffee in Granddad's cup laps out over the rim onto the saucer. "Who's it from?" *My God, I wonder if it's from Trevor. He left me a gift. Flowers, maybe.*

Granddad chortles. "Whoa, girl. I don't know."

I sprint into the hallway, grab the brown paper bag, run upstairs with it, and spill its contents onto my bed: a folded note, a red satin capelet, and a thin red *Girl Corps Handbook*. I grab the silky cape and bury my face in it. I hate that I wanted it to be from Trevor. Why do I even think like that?

With the cape still in my arm, I unfold the lined-paper note:

Dear Molly,

    We have a meeting on Thursday and a fund-raiser this Saturday.

    You have to join!!! You'll need these to be one of us!

Love,
Claire

It's sweet, actually. Seriously, that walk yesterday was the highlight of my weekend. Pathetic, maybe, but true. At least it made me forget about Trevor. Made me feel part of something outside myself. Unlike the Poseidon misadventure.

I hold the hardbound red Girl Corps book, and with one chipped blue fingernail I trace the shiny silver insignia on the cover, the compass with a heart nestled inside. Those girls yesterday exuded confidence, and I think that's what I felt when we finished the walk. Daddy said last night that I'd find myself, and I think I might be holding the map that will help me get there.

I don't let myself probe the *Girl Corps Handbook* right away because I want to take my time with it, so I finish my homework first. I place the mask Trevor made me in my sock drawer. I should break it, but I can't. Just like I haven't thrown away his old e-mails in the shoe box under my bed. Putting stuff away is about all I'm able to do, and that has to be good enough right now.

I delve into my work: a biology lab write-up, a take-home precalculus quiz, and a reading and rereading of act 1, scene 1 of Shakespeare's *Twelfth Night*.

That afternoon, when I'm finished, Uncle Murph pokes his bald head into my room. "You want to go to the grocery with me?" He winks. "You can push the trolley."

I giggle. When I was a kid, pushing the shopping cart was my favorite part of the whole outing.

"No thanks. I'm just going to relax."

"Okay, then. It's just not as fun without you."

When he leaves, I move from my desk to my bed and reach for the thin *Girl Corps Handbook*.

I'm not saying that I'm completely sold on the Girl Corps, but I do admit that whoever wrote that handbook knew how to cut to the chase. I pick up where I left off with Claire the other night when I read her to sleep. It's definitely what I call an easy read, say, cover to cover in an hour. Unlike Willy Shakespeare's stuff, which will take a generous chunk of a semester to wade through.

According to the *Girl Corps Handbook,* there are four Girl Corps core values, as shouted in my ear yesterday: Connection, Opinion, Resourcefulness, and Enlightenment . . . CORE. Sort of dorky, but it's a good way to remember each value.

Each year that a girl participates, she sets goals in each area, so that she "gains self-awareness and confidence." Qualities that "create responsible, confident, compassionate citizens" and that can only be realized through "self-reflection," for which "the Girl Journal is an important tool in giving girls a voice."

The Girl Journal section includes "one hundred journal starters to get you thinking about your core." I've never kept a journal before, although I've read a ton of novels written in journal form, as if they were secret diaries.

I guess I always worry that I have nothing to say, but I like the idea of the journal starters because I'll only have to answer questions. And there's no one to tell me if I answered right or wrong.

I scan the journal starters, which range from questions like *What does it mean to be a girl?* to *Whom do you admire, and why?* I stop, though, when I see number eleven: *What three items would you want with you if you were stranded on a desert island?* Emily must have been working through that one when she asked me on the walk yesterday. I avoided the question, whereas Emily seemed so confident about her answer.

From my desk I grab a blank seventy-page wide-ruled purple spiral-bound notebook and my pen of choice, a black Rolling Writer.

Girl Journal Entry One
QUESTION 11:
What three items would you want with you if you were stranded on a desert island?

If I were stranded on a desert island, I would be scared. I know that's not the question that was asked, but it's the answer that determines what I would want with me. I would need the comfort of things that make me calm. My family, for one, but I'm assuming I couldn't bring people with me or else it would totally take away from the desert island thing. So I would bring Buttons, because he's a part of my family and when I play him, I seem to forget reality, which would help me on a desert island. Especially if there were snakes and scorpions. I'd bring the statue of Mom, because when I hold it, it reminds me that there's a whole part of me that I don't even know, and it's comforting to me to think about who she was and that she was a good mother to me, that she loved me. I could also talk to the statue and that would make me feel less lonely. The third thing I would bring—

My phone rings and I flinch, like I really am on an island and the sound of its ring is out of place. I jump from my bed and grab it from its charger on my dresser.

It's a text, from Trevor. My hand shakes like I'm the castaway on the island who's holding her first found message in a bottle. It's one thing to have thought about Trevor these past couple of days, but now that he's trying to make contact with me, I'm desperate for it and open it like it's a script that will tell me what to do next.

SORRY. GOT STITCHES. FORGIVE U. U FORGIVE ME?

This is the chase I wanted the other night. He's reaching out, but forgive him? I lie back down on my bed and my thoughts spin around until I realize that I really am like a castaway on an island, afraid I'll never be found and that I'll always be alone. What if this is the only message I'll ever get?

If I don't respond, I might be alone for the rest of my life, without love. I should text him back, tell him to leave me alone, but I'm scared to completely let go of Trevor because I'm afraid I'll never feel the same way about anyone again.

I've liked him for seven years. Almost half my life. It's this castaway in me that feels the pull of him like a strong current that goes against everything I should be feeling.

I'm going to have to see him tomorrow at school. Even if I ignore him all day, I'll have to face him in ceramics sixth period. I want to be able to pretend he's not there, yet I want him to row his boat ashore and come back to me, crawling on his hands and knees.

I've got to get off this island, because in truth, I should want to throw a coconut at his head.

That night during open mike at the Banshee my phone vibrates for the second time in my pocket.

I can't look at it, because for the last few minutes, a toothless man named Hoots has been playing the spoons along my arm. I'm telling you, I will never sit on the edge of the booth again—it's easy access for this guy.

Daddy, the uncles, and Granddad clap along off-beat to encourage Hoots's tempo, which is the same as that of my vibrating phone. *Sorry, I can't come to the phone right now, an old man is rolling two tarnished table-spoons across my elbow!* I try to focus on the laughter and clapping around me.

Finally, Hoots segues over to his own knee and finishes off his ditty with a down-on-leg, up-on-palm beat. I peek at my phone: Trevor. Again!

Hoots is back, though. He gives a grand-finale *tick-tick-tick* on my shoulder and hoists his arms in the air. The almost full restaurant bursts into applause, like he's the American Idol of spoon players.

What does Trevor want? It was easier on Saturday, when there were no messages from him. It was final. But this . . . I'm not sure how to avoid something that's tugging my heart.

The crowd, which sits scattered at the tables and booths in the pub with plates of caraway scones and bowls of onion soup, begins to applaud more enthusiastically when Hoots leans over and kisses my cheek. "Thanks, doll," he says, and walks toward Aunt Tipper, who's at the bar holding out a pint for him. He might not have any teeth, but the guy sure is sweet.

"You're a good sport, Molly," Daddy says, giving me a hearty pat on the back.

"Thanks," I say. "I've always wanted someone to

play the spoons on me. It's like a dream come true, Daddy-O."

"Ha!" shouts Uncle Murph, raising his pint. The Guinness slops over the rim of the glass like a mini tidal wave. "Funny girl!"

I don't rush to read the text. Daddy's next to me, and I need to give Aunt Tip due props as she steps out from behind the bar and onto the stage to make an announcement. "We got more ramekins of onion soup coming out of the oven if you're interested. And please, give another round of applause for Hoots here, will ya?"

"Hear, hear, love!" shouts Clem, his tall, lanky body standing from our booth. The suit he's wearing looks like it's made of burlap. "Why don't you sing for us tonight, Tip?"

"Ha! It's been yonks since I sang. You know that."

"What do you say, folks? Don't you think the lady should sing?"

" 'Sright, Tip! Sing us a song!" yells Granddad.

Daddy sits next to me and leans over. "Your auntie, she loves to be begged into singing. She's going to milk this one."

"Yep," I say.

We watch as Aunt Tip raises her arms in the air, prolonging her performance. "Who's gonna man the bar?"

"I'll do it, Auntie Tip!" Uncle Garrett pushes out from the sticky oak table and walks over to the bar, but the truth is no one's gonna order a thing because Aunt Tipper's going to sing.

"I still see no reason for me to sing, though."

Clem straightens up, his body narrow like a pencil. "Tipper?"

"Yes, love?"

"Would you do it for a kiss?"

"Yes!" yells someone in the crowd.

"Depends who it's from," Aunt Tip says playfully.

"Well, from me, of course," says Clem. "I know I ain't no ride."

"You're not that bad," she says.

"So then?"

"I'll do it," she says with feigned annoyance. "Rourkey, come on up and play your guitar?"

Uncle Rourke moves toward the stage.

"You happy now, Clem?"

"Yes, Tip." He smiles, and you can see the love for her in his glossy eyes as he watches her with a tenderness beyond words. I want someone to love me like that. "This is for you, then, Clement." She leans down to Uncle Rourke, who's taken a seat on the short stool behind her onstage. He starts a finger-plucking progression to a song I don't recognize. Whereas before, the crowd was all hoots and hollers, there's a calm expectation, and then Aunt Tip begins to sing.

Aunt Tipper's voice is deep and steady, smooth, like a throat full of honey. The strum of Uncle Rourke's guitar is a soft tune beneath it.

"Come, come, come, love
Quickly come to me, softly move;
Come to the door, and away we'll flee,
And safe for aye will my darling be!
I wish, I wish, I wish in vain,
I wish I had my heart again. . . ."

I wish I had my heart again, too. Daddy puts his arm around me and gives me a squeeze. I hold his hand on my shoulder.

After the song is over, Aunt Tip bows and gives Uncle Clem a kiss.

I turn around to Daddy, who nods at Clem and Aunt Tip embracing in a hug. "I tell you," his voice cracks. "It's what I had with your mam, and it's worth every minute you have to wait for it. I know you liked that boy Trevor a lot, but remember that long loneliness is better than bad company, girl."

"I know, Daddy. It's just hard. It hurts. I wish I could just erase all my feelings for him, but they're still inside me."

"You got to go through those emotions whether you like it or not. It's part of the deal when you fall for someone, you get the bad with the good. It's the way it is in any relationship, for that matter."

"Right, but it feels more bad than good right now."

Daddy looks deep into my eyes. "That doesn't mean you'll never feel better. It just takes time, and then it's afterward that everything is understood. Right now, you're inside of it, so you've got to go through those feelings. Just like we did when your mom passed. You know as well as I that it still hurts, but you learn how to deal with those feelings. Part of dealing is going forward and living your life. Doing the things you love to do. The more you do those things, the more you realize life's worth living, even with the pain."

I wrap my arms around him and hug him tightly.

"Let's get up there with your uncle, shall we?" Daddy whispers in my ear.

"I'm just gonna grab Buttons," I say, pulling back from our hug so he can see me smile.

I run down the dim corridor plastered with W. B. Yeats poems and Van Morrison head shots, then duck into Aunt Tipper's office.

I open the text from Trevor: WE NEED 2 TALK.

I hear Daddy's voice. I've got to live my life, and right now, that means playing Buttons, not stepping into the cage with Trevor. Even so, I can't bring myself to delete the message.

Monday morning, 7:15 a.m., a car horn beeps.

I hoist my messenger bag over my shoulder and run down the steps toward the front door to meet Vanessa outside. Except for Granddad, the men in my house are gone by 6:45 each weekday. We only played a few songs last night, and got home early to prepare for the week ahead.

Parked in the driveway, in October's early-morning heat, I see Trevor's red Jeep, not Vanessa's blue tin-can car. My messenger bag slips down my arm. It hits the ground with a splat as though it were a large bird that's been shot off my shoulder.

The sight of him leaning against his car, his arms folded over his chest, makes me tingle, like I've just slathered myself in mint-flavored toothpaste. He doesn't deserve to be tingled for, but I don't know how to get rid of the feeling.

I didn't spend last night ignoring his text messages only to let myself collapse. I'm not going to let my emotions get in the way. Easier said than done, maybe, because my body trembles as he steps toward me on the path outside my door. A clear strip of medical tape is wrapped around his right earlobe, a sign that I did considerable damage.

Still, I'm betting it didn't hurt half as much as what he did to me. The tingling stops. He let me down and broke my heart! This is nothing to tingle about.

Trevor cautiously stops a few feet away from me. "Molly." His voice is soft, like it's wadded in cotton. "You can't ignore me forever."

"Leave me alone, Trevor." Now that's he closer, I notice the line of stitches beneath the tape, a crooked line. I'm suddenly reminded of Frankenstein's forehead.

"Why won't you hear me out?" Trevor asks.

The closer he gets to me, the more acute my hearing becomes. I hear his brown leather flip-flop scrape against the ground like a fingernail on a chalkboard. When I look him in the eyes, the same color as the dark-stained oak on the banister in my house, my own eyes become watery. I don't know how to talk or what to say. There should be plenty to say, but my tongue's swelled up in my mouth like a beached whale.

He takes my silence as an opportunity to explain. "I know you're pissed and I'm really sorry. I don't want to get back together with Felicia. But you've got to understand that we have a history. She's having a hard time letting go."

"You were *kissing* her." He can't deny what I saw through that window.

"I got caught up in the moment, okay? But I don't want to be with her."

"Actions speak louder than words." It's a lame and clichéd line, but it's all I've got right now. Besides, it also happens to be true.

Trevor shortens the distance between us even more—*scrape, scrape*—dragging his feet. He reaches out for my right hand, which turns to soft clay in his. I watch him, like he's holding someone else's hand, not mine, with its specks of leftover blue polish on the nails. "I'm here asking for forgiveness, aren't I? Doesn't *that* action say anything to you?"

My insides become hourglass sand spilling toward my feet. He smiles and I want to reach out and poke my finger in the pucker of his dimple with my free hand, like it's a reset button that will start at the beginning, before Friday, at the beginning of summer when everything was fresh and untainted.

Vanessa pulls up to the curb in her car. She spies me and Trevor on the walkway and yells out the passenger-side window. "Get in the car, Mol!"

Trevor looks in her direction. "I don't know how you stand her."

I pull my hand away from him. "She's my friend, Trevor." It's not until I turn around that I feel like I'm actually making an escape. When I get to Vanessa's car, she reaches over and opens the door for me. I duck inside and strap myself in.

The car screeches away from the curb. It takes every iota of strength for me not to look over my shoulder and see if Trevor is still standing there, gaping at me.

Vanessa turns off the music that was blaring in the car. "What was *he* doing here?" she asks.

"He came over to tell me he was sorry." I swallow hard. "I swear, Vanessa, I'm gonna lose it, you know? I'm trying to be strong and then I think, well, maybe he really is sorry."

Vanessa lets out a sarcastic-sounding chuckle. "I bet he's sorry."

"I don't understand what he wants. He acts like he didn't know what he was doing the other night."

"Don't you get it?" She takes her eyes off the road. "He wants you because at this point, he knows he can't have you."

My eyebrows raise. "So you think he's playing a game with me?"

"Don't you?"

I'd like to think that Trevor does want me. I even want to believe that he feels remorse. How stupid is that?

"I wouldn't have gone out with him in the first place if I thought he was a jerk." Vanessa could at least give me some credit.

"Still doesn't mean he's not a jerk, Molly. It just means that you weren't willing to see that part of him."

Sometimes I hate it when the girl makes sense.

Vanessa makes a curlicue in the air with her finger. "What's with this outfit?"

I'm wearing my mud-colored Banshee's Wake T-shirt, plain jeans, and slip-on tennies. No lipstick in my pocket. No mascara. Vanessa usually dresses like she's going clubbing or something. She's got a recipe of low-cut shirts and short skirts that she adheres to. I improvise a bit more with capris and jeans because most of the time I feel too clumsy in skirts. My legs are lanky, my hips too un-hippy. Anyway, I'd rather fly under the radar at school than call attention to myself these days.

"I'm just . . . lying low," I reply.

Hopefully this will satisfy her (but it probably won't).

Vanessa turns onto Marlborough Hill and the car engine strains with the incline. "Seriously, Molly, moping around and dressing like a slob isn't going to show Trevor you're over him."

I watch houses flash by out the window, the old, overgrown trees of South Hilldale disappearing as we ride through North Hilldale, the cleaner-cut neighborhood.

I can't help wondering if Vanessa is really trying to help me or if she's just talking out of her arse. Regardless, I'm not sure I can become a stronger person if she keeps cutting me down.

"How about some music?" I reach over and press play on the mp3 player, hoping this will be the perfect distraction from unwanted conversation. Razor Hurley screams out a lyric:

"You're in the backyard and I'm on the swing!
Come a little closer, baby, so you can feel my sting!"

I shake my head. "This song is so horrible, Nessa."

"Yeah, they do kind of suck, don't they?"

"So you just realized this?"

"No, I came to that conclusion after Karl burped while we were making out and it tasted like garlic."

I snort out a laugh. "That is so disgusting!"

"I know. And my mom got home last night with take-out spaghetti and I was like, 'Uh, thanks, Mom. Not hungry.'" Vanessa reaches over and presses a few buttons on the player. "Let's hear something else."

I couldn't agree with her more, but I have to admit, I wish my best friend would actually hear *me*.

Girl Journal Entry Two

QUESTION 46:

How do the choices you make now affect your future? Explain.

I may not answer this question the way I am supposed to, but I saw the word *choice* and it reminded me of something Uncle Murph always says, that we can do anything we want in our lives with the exception of one detail: we can't choose not to die. At some point, we have to die. Other than that, we get to make any choice we want about anything.

But I think he's overlooking something important. There's one other thing that I doubt is much of a choice: you can't really choose to stop loving someone, either.

You can stop calling, delete them from speed dial. You can ignore them, turn your head in the crowded shuffle of passing period when you see the fleck of orange from your favorite T-shirt of his. You can write inside wide-ruled lines of this Girl Journal hoping the black ink curves of your sloppy penmanship will be a distraction from thinking about that person. (Not working, because the vision of Trevor leaving ceramics at the end of sixth period, brushing by me as if I were an anonymous anybody in a room full of people, still rattles around in my head.)

But you don't really have a choice to pluck someone you love or really like out of your heart.

Like a mother.

Like Trevor.

I've spent the last three nights searching on the Internet for how-to-get-over-someone advice and here's what I found:

- Forget about them. (Without some thought-removal vacuum, I don't see how this is possible.)
- Focus on someone else. (Rebound, baby!)
- Erase/bury/burn mementos of the person.
- Fill your time with things to do. (Get a life, Loser!)

One person even said it takes double the time you were with someone to get over them, which gives me till April. What am I supposed to do in the meantime?

. . .

To avoid Trevor, I spend the first part of the week tramping through the obstacle course of Hilldale High, darting around sharp corners of mazelike hallways and skipping art class. However, I'm not as skilled in avoiding Girl Corps–related drama, which erupts on Thursday night in front of Faith's Power Community Church.

Three hours ago, Dede asked me to babysit Claire after school while she went to Pilates class. A half hour ago, Claire begged me to come with her to her Girl Corps meeting and I said sure (because frankly, I had a good time at the walk, I enjoy writing in that silly journal, and I like the attention that the little girls paid me). One minute ago, we pulled into the church parking lot, and now, here I am, having what seems like a panic attack. A gigantic lump has formed in my throat.

"The meeting is in a church?" I ask Dede as a baby lump hatches on the existing lump, making it impossible to swallow. The last time I was in one was at Mom's memorial. I have a strong feeling that I might cry and shriek or puke and faint. I'd rather be anywhere than here, even back at Trevor's house, watching him and Felicia go at it again.

Dede shakes her head. "No, the meetings are in the multipurpose room." She points to the building on our right, separate from the church. Claire jumps out of the car and holds the door open for a few of her friends we picked up along the way.

"C'mon, Molly!" she shouts. "Rhondi won't like it if we're late."

Rhondi is the least of my problems. I'm frozen in the front seat. "I didn't know Girl Corps was a religious thing."

Dede places a gentle manicured hand on my knee. Aunt Tip has man hands; Dede's are soft and look well moisturized. "There's no religion involved in the Corps whatsoever. It's just that the church allows the girls to meet here, free of charge. It's *only* the multipurpose room. They've never gone into the chapel."

I look at the building. It's one story. No high ceiling. No angels flapping their wings. "I'm sorry," Dede says. "I had no idea that you had a—" She stumbles, and I'm unable to help her because I'm not sure what to call it, either. God phobia? Church jitters? Amazon-sized fear of churchly places?

"You want me to go in with you?"

"No, I'm okay." I realize I'm being ridiculous, and I don't want to jeopardize Dede's trust in my mental health. She's the closest thing to an employer I have right now. "I'm fine."

I follow the girls past the gargantuan wooden cross that stands guard at the entryway. It's not judging me, I tell myself. In fact, it's never seen me before, and it's not the same cross that was inside Saint Didacus Church the day of Mom's memorial service, although it may be a distant relative. I keep walking.

Within ten minutes of our arrival, I'm at ease. The

room is generic, like a classroom except without the maps of the world, evacuation charts, and spitballs. It even has the same stale-paste smell as a classroom. I let out a sigh of relief.

After sitting through the singing of the rhyming anthem, and the announcements (which include details about an upcoming fund-raiser involving jarring jam and an annual campout), we begin an "enlightenment" session. Thankfully, Rhondi hasn't even flinched at my presence here. Maybe she's under the impression that I've joined Girl Corps, which just might happen because I haven't thought of Trevor once while I've been here. Except for just now.

I'm also curious about getting to know this Rhondi woman. I found out the following information about her while babysitting Claire:

Her last name is Papadiamantopoulos. (Yikes.)

She is divorced and has a son who attends community college nearby.

She loves her cat, Arnold.

She has been involved in Girl Corps since she was Claire's age. (Talk about commitment!)

"Tonight we're going to focus on stranger danger." Rhondi whips out a felt board from a massive Mary Poppins–sized bag and speaks for ten uninterrupted minutes via felt-people theater. She dangles a gangly felt man in front of a felt little girl wearing a pink felt dress who screams, "No, Mister! Fire! Fire!"

I can only imagine the gangly felt man as Trevor. And me as the felt girl, wearing a more comfortable ensemble of sweatshirt and jeans, yelling, "Yes! Yes!" Pathetic.

After storyboard theater, Rhondi prepares us for our assignment. "Most of you are familiar with my son, Michael." There are gleeful giggles on the carpet. "Michael has agreed to come and be our stranger. I'm confident he will make a good one, as he is a star thespian in his freshman class theater department at Hilldale Community College."

Hatsuku raises her hand.

"Yes, Hatsuku?"

"What's a lespian?" Without success, I try to cover up my laughter with a cough.

Rhondi glares my way. "A *thes*pian," she corrects Hatsuku, "is an actor or actress." She looks at me smugly, like she's an adult who can handle such a slipup without laughing at the innocent cuteness of it.

Now I know another thing about Rhondi: the lady has to lighten up.

We're told to get into pairs and role-play a "stranger-danger" situation with our partner. At the end of our "practice" we are going to perform for the entire group with Michael as our "stranger."

Rhondi pairs me with Emily, my diminutive brace-faced hippie girl, who wears a knitted rainbow-colored cap and a shirt that says ANYTHING BOYS CAN DO, GIRLS CAN DO BETTER!

"I like your T-shirt," I say.

"Thanks. My mom got it for me."

"She must be a cool person."

"She's a political activist," she says nonchalantly. "She hates to cook and thinks the United States is run by male chauvinists."

"Well, she sounds interesting."

"She is. She has a lot of opinions."

I chortle. "I have a friend who's like that."

"Really?"

"Yep. She'll tell you how it is even if you beg her not to tell you."

"She and my mom sound a lot alike."

Emily looks over at Rhondi, who gives me a stink-eyed *Get going* look.

Emily plays a very convincing stranger. She pretends to offer me candy out of her cupped hand. "Want some gourmet jelly beans? They're imported from Candy Land."

In my best squeaky girl voice I say, "Fire."

She shakes her head at my lame performance. "I don't think your voice is loud enough, Molly. You really need to say it like you mean it. You should try it again."

"Well, Emily," I say. "I accept your challenge and will show you that this girl's not gonna fall for the ol' gourmet jelly bean lure." I cough to clear my vocal cords, then scream at full force, "Fire!"

The room plummets to impressive silence.

Rhondi's body language so far has been pretty easy

to read. She's got a general pissed-off air about her that can be seen through the eternal glare that makes you wonder if both of her eyes are made of glass. Except at this moment, while silence hangs over the room, she half-cocks an eyebrow at me. If I didn't know any better, I might assume she's impressed with the way I executed the word *fire*. Maybe the woman isn't made of stone after all.

She turns to resume her coach work with Hatsuku and Maribel. Voices rise into the background again. "So," I say to Emily. "How was I?"

Emily's face lights up in a full-toothed silver smile. "You did it."

"Thanks," I say, feeling good about it myself. "You're a good director, Emily." She nods with pride.

Five minutes into practice, Michael arrives, cloaked in black, a sharp contrast to his peaches-and-cream pale skin. He doesn't look that much like his mother, which I guess isn't a bad thing, really. In fact, he seems irritated and flustered, as though he's been coerced into being here by someone who means a lot to him. Given my personal history, I can't help sympathizing with the guy.

I sit with the girls on the carpet to begin the role-play. Hatsuku and Maribel volunteer to go first. As they choreograph their places on the linoleum squares outside the carpet, my phone vibrates in my pocket. I'm so glad I had the brains to turn off the ringer. Rhondi's head would spin 360 degrees if my phone interrupted the stranger-danger performance.

In an opportune moment while Rhondi is coaching the performers—"Louder!" and "Again! He'd take you!"—I flip open my phone in my lap and steal a glance at the screen. Text. From Trevor. A whoosh of heat flushes over me. WHY R U DOING THIS?

My heart has been trapped in a birdcage all week. It'd be one thing if the cage door were shut and there were no way out, but what makes it so hard is that the little door is open and I have to keep everything inside with my own willpower. I'm not sure how much longer I can hold back.

"Molly!" Rhondi whips her head in my direction. "No electronic devices during Girl Corps."

"Sorry."

"No." She wags her finger. "Action, Molly. Turn off the phone." Her tone softens. "We are what we do, not what we say."

I turn off my phone, but the keypad in my head is already tapping out an answer.

Trevor asked a stupid question. He has been ignoring me all week in response to me ignoring him. It's like an ignoring-fest. And the bottom line is that he cheated, and if he were really sorry, he'd be at my feet every day begging for forgiveness instead of giving up so easily. Not that I want to get back together with him, because I know that's wrong, even though that's what part of me wants. I'll take it from Rhondi: we are what we do.

"Molly and Emily?" Rhondi calls to us. We stand up from the nubby carpet.

"Molly," Rhondi says as we approach the front, "you take your turn first."

What? "Oh, um, I thought I was just helping Emily practice her role-playing so she'd be ready for Michael." Michael rubs his ear, seemingly embarrassed for me.

Rhondi doesn't say a word and instead offers an icy glare.

"Sure," I say. "I'll go ahead and take my turn."

Emily grabs my hand. "You can do it."

"Thanks, Em."

"Yay, Molly!" Claire yells and claps. The other girls join in the clapping. "Go, Molly! Go!"

"Girls! Quiet down, please." I don't like that whenever the girls shower me with some sugar, she has to stop them, as if she's jealous.

I face Thesbo, who says, "Curtain," which evidently means we're starting.

Thesbo Michael (whimpering): Could you help me find my puppy?

Me: No.

Thesbo: Why don't you just come over to my car (head nod toward invisible car) so I can show you a picture of the puppy? (His voice breaks and cracks under the intense pressure.)

Me: No!

For a moment, Michael is not the squeamish son of Rhondi I know him to be. I imagine that he is looking at me with that hopeful gleam in his eye, the one I recognize from Trevor. The one that says, *Please. I'll do anything for you, just say yes.* It's the kind of look that can get a girl into trouble. The kind of look that causes a girl to lose her head and convinces her to do something she doesn't want to do. *WHY R U DOING THIS?* Is Trevor screwing with my head?

I step toward Thesbo so that I'm close enough to see speckles of sweat glisten on his upper lip. The words race out of my mouth before I can stop them, my heart sputtering inside me.

"Fire!"

The audience claps. But I don't feel finished just yet. I shake my head at Thesbo Michael.

"All you guys think you can con us with candy. Or puppy dogs. Or sweet talk!" Thesbo looks confused and annoyed, which feeds my fury. "But you won't be there once we take the bait!" My voice gets louder. "You'll cheat! And lie! And only think about sex! And—"

"Stop! Stop it right there!" Rhondi points an unmanicured fingernail at me. "Molly, *outside.*"

What? What did I do?

Was it something I said?

One glance at the girls and their dropped jaws tells me it was. What *did* I say? My short-term memory is totally zapped.

I glance down at the girls sitting on the carpet; their gaping mouths look like frozen yawns. Sophia raises a stiff arm in the air just as Rhondi starts to take me outside. "What is it, Sophia?" Rhondi asks impatiently.

"Are we allowed to say 'sex'?" she asks in a catty voice.

"No!" says Rhondi. "Michael, do a soliloquy or something for the girls. I'll be right back."

I turn back to Thesbo Michael, who observes me with wholehearted apology on his face, as if our scene together were real and he's remorseful about not having a puppy to show me after all.

Outside the church Rhondi and I stand underneath the looming cross. I turn, so that the cross is behind me and I don't have to be reminded of something that's too scary to remember.

Rhondi stares at me with hands on her hips, tapping her foot expectantly. I wonder if this is what my own mother would have looked like when she was disappointed in me.

In a measured tone she says, "I thought I was fine with you being here. And I really think you might learn a thing or two. But if you're going to mock our organization, you're out. Don't come back."

"I'm not mocking, Rhondi. I'm sorry. I've got a lot on my mind and I really didn't mean to go off on Michael like that."

"It's not him I'm worried about," she snaps. "It's the girls. You must be careful with your words. That was inappropriate language back there. Language of which I doubt the parents would approve."

I don't argue with her, because the shock on their faces back in that room said it all. I wanted to be here, but I didn't think I'd be seen as a bad influence. "I'm sorry, I'll leave." I don't want to, but I can't seem to obtain her approval.

She gives me a head-to-foot scan. "That's a common theme with you, isn't it?"

"No, it just seems like you don't want me here."

"I didn't say that. You have plenty to learn from these girls, Molly. But you need to keep it G-rated. This isn't some joke. It's real girls learning real values."

But this is so not a G-rated world. There are strangers on the prowl baiting kids with lies, and evil dictators not feeding their own people. There are boys out there who'll tell you they love you and then cheat. There's even the possibility that there's a God who's willing to take away your own mother.

"I don't want to leave, Rhondi. I—I need this right now." I'm confused, and I've never had anything like Girl Corps. It makes me feel like I have the opportunity to be a better person and learn who I'm supposed to be.

Rhondi's arms fall to her sides, and the tense lines of her forehead soften. She's no fairy godmother, but at least she has calmed down.

"If you're serious about being in the Corps, you have some soul-searching to do, young lady." Soul-searching? "To be honest, I think you older girls need the Corps more than these young ones. At least they are willing and eager to learn how to respect themselves."

I want answers, too. I want to know how to search for my soul.

"You have a copy of the handbook?"

I nod.

"There's some crucial journal prompts—sixty through seventy—that focus on goal setting. Self-improvement doesn't come without introspection."

"I haven't gotten to those yet, but I did start a Girl Journal," I reply, hoping she'll see that I'm not completely without a backbone.

Rhondi doesn't even bother to act surprised that I've written in the journal. I wonder if she's the kind of woman you can ever impress or if there's an infinite number of hoops to jump through. Regardless, I don't want her angry with me.

"Keep writing in the journal. It's going to help you sort through who you are and who you want to be. But it will only work if you follow through—that's the other half of the battle."

"I'll try."

"No." Her voice turns firm. "You will or you won't."

"I will."

"Good. Now, the next time you feel like you're going to explode, think SCAB."

"SCAB?" Um, that sounds gross.

"It's a process. First, stop what you're doing. Then, count to ten. Next, act—get your body moving. And finally, don't forget to breathe."

"What does that do?"

"It keeps your emotions in check, Molly. Go ahead, do it."

"Now?"

"Yes. How do you expect it to work if you don't do it?"

"But I'm not . . . emotional at this moment."

She sighs. "I know, but it'll be easier to remember if you do it. So much of who we are is what we do. So *stop*."

I raise my arms out to my sides. "I'm stopped."

"*Count* to ten."

I feel like an idiot, but hell, if this is supposed to guide me to personal victory, I'm happy to do it. "One, two—"

"Silently," she says, impatience rattling her voice. "Counting to yourself helps you focus on something besides lashing out with your emotions. Picture each number as you count."

I close my eyes to envision the curves and lines of each number as I count. Straight one . . . curly three . . . swirly eight . . .

"Now, *act*—a simple action that keeps you focused."

I open my eyes, then reach down and pick up a leaf from the ground.

"Good. All you need is a simple action. You can walk, clean up, whatever, and as you're going through that action—the simple action of getting your body redirected—focus on breathing. *Breathe.* That's 'B.' In and out. In and out."

Breathing is one thing I know how to do. Thank God.

"That, Molly, is SCAB. It's a technique that will help you with your emotions."

"Is it a Girl Corps thing?" I don't remember seeing it in the handbook.

"No, it helps with anxiety. I use it all the time with my patients."

"You're a doctor?" This never dawned on me. Probably because I'm not used to her bedside manner.

"No, I'm an occupational therapist. I help rehabilitate people who need help functioning in this world." She must have a lot of patients. "Now let's get back in that room." She walks forward, not looking back.

I stand for a second under the cross and picture the Girl Corps insignia with the heart inside a compass. A symbol to make these girls think that the world will abide by the lessons they learn, if they follow their own path, their own hearts.

I can't say that it's not possible. In fact, I'm hoping it is. It may be a false sense of hope, but maybe there is some of my mother in me. She hoped to find a better life here in the United States, so she took the risk and left the life she knew behind. There's a spark in me that wants something more than I have, too, and that's what makes me step toward the multipurpose room, filled with, of all things, purpose.

On Friday at 7:15 a.m. Vanessa beeps her horn. I skip downstairs into the empty kitchen and grab a bruised banana. When I duck into the car, Vanessa slams on the gas pedal before I've put on my seat belt. She glances over at me.

"Hey, Tootsie Pop, why didn't you call me back last night?" she asks.

"If you can't tell from the bags under my eyes, I had a late night." The buckle makes a clicking sound and I'm strapped in. "I didn't get home from the Girl Corps meeting until eight, then I had to do my English synopsis and—"

"Whoa—slow down a minute, sista."

"What? I was just gonna say that I was up past midnight studying for precalc."

"No, you said that you went to a Girl Corps meeting."

"No, I didn't." Did I? Stupid sleep deprivation!

"Yes, you did."

"Look, I had to babysit and then Claire begged me to go to the meeting. I couldn't say no." Things have been more and more tense with Nessa. I feel like I have to defend myself to her all the time. She doesn't understand why I can't erase Trevor from my head. It's not likely she's going to understand the Corps.

"Did you wear the cape?" Vanessa inquires with a grin.

"No! I told you, I went because Claire wanted me to."

"Whatever," she says with a smile. "You don't have to get defensive about it."

I lean back against the headrest and wish there were an eject button, like the kind for the glass elevator in *Charlie and the Chocolate Factory,* so that I could just press it and catapult out of the car.

All of a sudden, Vanessa's finger aims at the bull's-eye of my sweatshirt. "You wore that Monday, you know."

"I don't care." At least, I thought I didn't.

"Well, it certainly shows."

My head swivels to the side slowly and I try to shoot one of Rhondi's glass-eyed stares at her. But Vanessa is immune to it. She just sticks out her tongue and wiggles it at me. I reach down to one of the many available silver gum wrappers littering the floor and flick it at Vanessa's head. She laughs, and finally, so do I.

"I'm gonna say something, and I'm not kidding, Molly, okay?"

"Okay."

"Even though it might be seen as sorta silly that you went to a Girl Corps meeting, it's what I love about you. You're kind, Mollers." She scrunches her eyes into cavewoman mode. "Me think you do good by people."

"Thank you, Nessa. Me think that might be the nicest thing you've ever said to me."

With that, she turns on the stereo and I'm thankful that the ride to school ends on a good, loud note.

The sleeves of Ms. Pinkwater's shirt are particularly flowy today, so when she raises her arms to dictate instructions during sixth-period ceramics, it's hard not to visualize her floating in midair. "Today is your last chance to glaze. If your project didn't go to the kiln Wednesday, it'll need to go in at the end of class for critique on Monday."

When I got to class, Trevor disappeared into the kiln. I didn't see him during lunch, and I wonder if this is the same Trevor who texted me yesterday. Evidently, there's an apologetic phone Trevor and a churlish in-the-flesh Trevor. I don't know which one is real.

"Any questions?" asks Ms. Pinkwater. *I'm here to learn art,* I tell myself in an attempt to wipe away Trevor like he's a smudge on the window of my mind. We are what we do, and I've got to get doing. On Wednesday I finally molded my project into something recognizable.

It's a foot, and it's ready to be glazed, so I go to my cubby, grab my dried foot, and bring it over to the glazing station.

Because I am not intuitively gifted, I have to read the glazing instructions poster on the wall to interpret the plastic buckets of oozy glaze, which all look similar, like dark shades of nail polish, the spectrum ranging from plum to dark chocolate.

"It's easiest to go in order of the bucket labels," says Justin Kubilnicky, whose hair flips up in front like a mini visor. "Just make sure you don't mix those glazes"—he points to a grouping of buckets numbered with ones—"*after* those." Now he points to the number-two buckets.

"Ohhh," I say. "You must think I'm brilliant, seeing that I couldn't even figure out the obvious."

"Nah." He sniffs. "Sometimes the most obvious things are the most confusing."

"You need that first, though," Trevor interrupts from behind. Justin backs away toward his own table, while Trevor reaches over me and points at a bucket labeled "primer." Involuntarily, my heart twitters like the blind bird that it is.

The mesh strip on his earlobe is crusted over with dried scab. Black stitches poke out from behind. "You have to prime it first," he says in a soft voice, "so it doesn't crack."

He disappears as smoothly as he showed up, leaving me alone, but I still feel the aftershock of him. He only gave me advice about the glazing process, but it's the delivery that got me. Soft, smooth. It's the same pitch he uses when he whispers in my ear. The last whisper having been "I love you."

Right, and I'm supposed to stay focused. Thankfully, I'm at school, so globbing into a little ball on the floor and sobbing isn't an option. No, instead, I paint each toenail of my ceramic foot a different color. By the time Ms. Pinkwater chimes the Tibetan bowl, I'm the last to put my project into the kiln, but I'm satisfied that I've finished.

Except when I reach the cavern of the kiln, Trevor's in it, organizing like he's supposed to do before a firing. He squats down and shuffles some projects around on the bottom shelf. "Hey," he says, as though we haven't spent the entire week ignoring each other. "Just set it up there on the top shelf. You're tall enough to reach it."

Is that supposed to be a compliment or is he trying to say I'm too tall? I walk over and, on tiptoe, slide my ceramic foot into a tight space between something that looks like an ashtray and another flat slab of something.

"You didn't answer my text." He scrapes a piece of reddish clay from his palm. It is completely unreasonable that Trevor is allowed to look so good right now. Aside from his ear, everything—from his perfectly clipped, clay-encrusted fingernails to the way his gleaming eyebrow hairs arch smoothly over his brown eyes—is flawless. My mind draws a blank because my heart is pounding—*pum, pum, pum!*—in my ears. Is this stranger danger without the jelly beans and puppies? I'm immobile. Couldn't even yell "fire" if I wanted.

"Molly?" Now he's locked me into his gaze. His hand runs through his hair. He steps closer to me—I hear the *scrape, scrape, scrape* of his feet above the dusty kiln floor. Underneath my Banshee T-shirt, my stomach and heart collide.

"We should hang out tonight," he says. "And talk."

"Fire!" Yell "fire!" But I don't say anything. What is it I want to say? I honestly don't know. That could be the problem, or the point—there are no words. Except for SCAB, but I can't remember what the acronym stands for. Bah!

The bell rings. "I've got to go, Trevor."

I run out of the kiln toward my messenger bag and sprint out the door toward the mouth of the parking lot. It's not fair! I want to hate him, but there's that part of me that can't let go and is already accepting the offer to hang out tonight. Maybe I'm a coward for running away, but even Rhondi said one foot in front of the other. It's all I can do.

My feet slap the pavement past the wave of people pouring out of classrooms. Daddy's voice echoes in my head: "Move on with your life, Molly."

I catch my breath in the parking lot, thankful that Nessa and I were early to arrive this morning and that Trevor's red Jeep is parked at the opposite end. I walk over to Vanessa, who's waiting for me in her car. Before

I get in, I wipe my face with my hand and breathe, getting a lungful of exhaust.

I won't mention what happened with Trevor. Nessa would be glad I walked away, but I couldn't tell her that Trevor seemed sincere about wanting to talk to me. I'm not up for another anti-Trevor speech. The kind that makes me feel stupid for having been with him in the first place and even stupider for still holding feelings for him.

I'm proud of myself, though. Tiny little victory fists go up in my head. If Rhondi were here—not that I'd want her here—she might give me some credit for doing the right thing and walking away, à la stranger danger.

Once I'm inside the car, Vanessa cranks up Radiohead on the stereo. "It's Friday, Mollers!" She shifts us into reverse, but before she spins out of her space, someone pounds on the roof of the tiny car. She slams on her brakes. "What the—!"

"Bo," I say, pointing over her shoulder to Bo Burns, tall yet slouchy, manly and stubbly, part bear, part guinea pig, just outside her window.

"Ah, there." She turns down the volume and opens her window to talk to him. "Thanks for making me think my car was being attacked by a giant ape." She's actually not that far off the mark.

"Got your attention, didn't I?" He leans down, peeking his bushy-eyebrowed head into the car to give me a wave. "Hey, Molly."

"Hey." Vanessa tried to hook me up with Bo before

Trevor and I became an item. Not to be mean or anything, but Bo—who I witnessed at a party last year completely drunk and playing air guitar to some Metallica song on top of Brian Metcalf's built-in barbecue—just doesn't do it for me. And the geometry textbook he's hugging in his sturdy-looking arm doesn't have me fooled.

"You working tonight, Vanessa?"

"Till eight. You?"

"Nah. But, uh, Cooper really wants to hang out with you." He makes a *click-click* sound with his tongue to inform Vanessa of the hubba-hubba factor involved in this information.

"Really?" Vanessa says. "That's cool." I know Cooper wanting to hang out with Vanessa is *more* than cool for her. Last year I was her escort on an excursion to True Value Hardware so she could drool over Cooper shelving paint gallons. "Cooper Havener," to quote Nessa, who was practically breathless near a display of interior paint swatches, "is a beefy blond yum-yum cake." Unquote. I love Ness when she's bubbly like that, as opposed to explosive.

"Well, definitely, let's hang out." Vanessa gives Bo an instant RSVP. "Why don't you come over to my place?" Vanessa can always count on her mom being out on a Friday night.

"Cool," he says. "Call me on my cell after work." Vanessa nods. "Later, then." He cranes his neck to get an eyeful of me. "Bye, Molly. See you tonight." His fist gives one last pound on Vanessa's car before he struts into parking lot sprawl.

"Yesss!" Vanessa says. She scoops her shoulder up to her face coyly. "Cooper wants to hang out with me! Meow, meow, meow!"

"I'm so not up to going out, Vanessa."

"Relax, we're not going out, we're just gonna be at my house. It'll be good for you. And, if you didn't notice, Bo is totally absorbed with you. I smell a rebound man." In a low, lusty voice she says, "He wants you, Mol."

"Well, I'm not into him, okay? Remember: need break, no males? You being supportive of that?"

"This isn't like Lent or something. *You* have a choice." She snaps her fingers in the air. "Trevor's history."

I stand firm. I walked away from Trevor—ran, if you want to get technical. I can do this, too. It's about self-respect and voice and opinion. "Did you hear me, Nessa? I'm not going."

She sticks her tongue out at me again. "Party pooper."

And for the first time I take one of her put-downs as a compliment.

Nessa drops me off at the Banshee after school; it's been months since I've spent a Friday reveling in Bangers, Beans, and Battle of the Bands. Had I been a more decent daughter, granddaughter, and niece over these last few months, I would have sacrificed a few Friday nights away from Trevor and pizza to bond with my family. It's not without a pang of sadness that I realize Trevor and his couch are no longer a Friday-night-venue possibility.

I spend the afternoon on a barstool refilling saltshakers, which offers the challenge of a carnival booth game. Just as I can never aim right to get the Ping-Pong ball into a floating vase, I can't manage to pour salt from the silver beak of the blue container into the small orifice of the glass shaker without creating an overflow of salt at the lip. There are more sand dunes of salt on the countertop than inside the shakers, but Aunt Tip doesn't seem to mind, because she rewards me with a napkin full of roasted cashews that she's warmed up for me in the oven.

When Granddad arrives around five, we eat a meal of bangers and beans. As a kid, I didn't like the beans part, so I'd stab the sausages from the bowl and arrange them on a side plate to eat. But now the mingling of the two textures—mild creamy beans with juicy grilled sausage—swimming in the smoky tang of the sauce makes for a happy mouth.

By eight o' clock I'm at the bar, tapping two plastic sword toothpicks together. Daddy and the uncles aren't here yet. Aunt Tip waves me away with her soggy bar cloth. "Molly B, you've got to scoot over to a table now. It's getting crowded here."

"I'll go check on Granddad, then." I leave my barstool, where the underage are forbidden, and sit next to Granddad at the booth where we ate dinner, which has become the sign-up station for tonight's competition. A few hours earlier, his hair was tame. Now it looks like thick tufts of spiderwebs.

"You ready, Molly B? Clem and I got stiff competition tonight. Look here." He holds up the yellow legal pad that serves as the evening's Battle of the Bands roster and taps it with a porky finger. "Eight bands have signed up."

"Impressive. That's got to be good for business."

Granddad gives me a wink. "Clem and me play better with more fire under our bellies, too."

"Okay!" Clem shouts, the thin line of his pipe-cleaner-shaped body onstage. "We're gonna start the night with Malcolm Gallagher and his bagpipes." Malcolm, who looks like he's over a hundred years old, with snowball white hair and a slow, scuffing walk, shuffles from his table to the stage with his bagpipes, its siphons and tubes splaying out in all directions like the legs of an octopus.

It's when Clem calls the next act up to the stage that I spot Vanessa standing at the entrance to the Banshee.

I don't wave my hands up in the air so she can spot me right away. Instead, I take a rare moment to watch her like an outsider. She holds her car keys in one hand and bites her lip as she scans the crowd to find me. Her eyes are rimmed in her favored dark smudge of eyeliner.

She must have gone home to change after work, because she's wearing a short black skirt with leggings underneath and a yellow V-neck shirt that completely complements her dark complexion. She is really a beautiful girl, which explains why she's always managed to turn heads.

Agnes Flynn, who teaches Irish dancing on Monday nights, is up onstage with a drum strapped to her shoulder, and as she starts to tap-tap-tap on it, I approach Vanessa, hoping her plans with Cooper fell through. It'd be nice if she were here to simply hang out with me, except she's searching for me too intently for that.

She spots me walking toward her and presses her hands together in thanks.

"Hey, Ness. You here for bangers and beans?" Vanessa used to come here with me often when we were younger. We'd spend time in the kitchen, eating warm PB and J's and drinking cold milk to our hearts' content.

"I need you something fierce, Mol," she says with a pout. "Come look."

I'm not surprised. I knew this was coming, but even so, I'm disappointed that she needs me.

I follow her out into the long hallway and through the heavy door of the Banshee.

Once we get outside, she points to her car across the street. "See, there?" Cooper sits on the passenger side. A clear outline of Bo is visible in the backseat. He's too tall for it and is forced to slump hunchback style, like an ox shoved into a baby stroller.

"Jasmine couldn't make it, and I *seriously* need you."

I can't believe this. She really doesn't care about me. "But I told you earlier, I want to be here at the Banshee tonight."

"I know, Mollers." She grabs my hand in the warmth of her own. "This is not about me trying to get you to do something you don't want to do. This is about asking you to do your pal a favor."

"No." I pull my hands away from her. "Go without me." I hate that I sound like I don't care, but I'm trying to be strong for myself here, too. If I'm going to stand my ground, she's got to learn to go it alone.

"Not with two guys. I won't get a chance to have Cooper to myself. Please, Molly. You don't have to do anything with Bo, just visit. He's funny *and* double-jointed." I offer a forced laugh. "He'll keep you entertained!"

"Thanks, but I told you, I can't." She's got to listen to me!

She gets down on her knees. I cross my arms and look away. "Molly, please. I'm begging you. I won't drink or anything, so if we get to my house and you're uncomfortable, I will take you home."

"Like you did when I wanted to leave the Poseidon? C'mon, Ness. You have to go without me."

"But this is different."

It's not. I'm about ready to turn around and walk back into the Banshee.

"Mol? *Please*. Don't give up on me now. I've never needed you more."

And it happens. That thing when I give in to her. She's my best friend. I've been here at the Banshee for hours. No one here really needs me. Nessa does, though. When I weigh what I want against my friendship with Nessa, the friendship part always tips the scale. I don't turn and look at her just yet. "You *promise* you'll bring me home if I want to leave?"

"Promise, Mol. Now, please, please?"

"I'm going inside to tell my granddad I'm leaving with you." I turn. "You better tell Bo I have no interest in him, Nessa."

She showers me with kisses on my face. "Molly, you're the best."

Bo and I sit on Vanessa's velvety rust-colored couch in the living room of her two-bedroom apartment, which is located in my part of town, South Hilldale. The small, two-story stucco building looks like the product of a child who plunked one beige block on top of another.

Inside the apartment the walls reflect the current interior design trend: dark colors. Hence brown-mustard walls encase Bo and me, like we're tucked inside a deli sandwich.

Vanessa and Cooper make out in the kitchen, which has the color and shine of eggplant skin; Vanessa sits on top of the white tiled counter, right above the dishwasher. Her legs wrap around Cooper, who stands with his head dangerously close to pots and pans that hang from a rack on the ceiling.

Overall, it's been uneventful, just how I want it.

Bo's into his *fifth* beer, while I slurp a Diet Coke. Bo starts waxing poetic about comic books. "Iron Man rocks!" He flattens his palms to simulate the comic book hero's "repulsor beams," which shoot from his gloved suit.

I laugh. This guy is no predator. Vanessa was right about him being entertaining.

Dull fluorescent light from the kitchen casts an eerie glow on Bo.

"Nessa said you're double-jointed?" I ask.

"You want to see?"

"I think so."

He reaches over and plunks his wet mouth on mine. Bo tastes sour, like a leftover stewed carrot. I nudge him away and wipe the slobber from my lips. "What'd you do that for?" I'll never again ask a guy if he's double-jointed.

Bo leans into me, toward my ear. His stubble scratches my chin on his way there. He whispers, "I'm sorry. I heard about Trevor cheating on you. I'm not like that."

I push him back again, my palm firm on his heaving chest. "What did you say?"

"I'm not a cheater."

"No, how did you know that Trevor cheated on me?"

"Um, Vanessa?"

I crane my neck so I can see Vanessa and Cooper in the kitchen, where Cooper's hand frisks underneath her shirt. Did she try to set me up, here? And who is she to go and tell hairy Bo about my private life?

Bo pulls back, blows air puffer fish–style out his lips. "That's cool," he says. He arches his back, wipes his forearm against his lips, runs his fingers through his hair. "I can wait."

He's going to be waiting a long time. "I'm sorry. I'm not into hooking up with anyone right now." I look back over to Vanessa. "Ness?" She doesn't hear me. "Vanessa!"

She peels out of her lip fusion with Cooper. "Yeah?" She looks over Cooper's shoulder, her legs still wrapped around him. Cooper kisses her neck because her lips aren't free right now.

"You have to take me home."

Bo fishes around his pocket and reels in a set of keys. "I can take you home." He's a car wreck waiting to happen; plus, it's time for Vanessa to keep her word.

This is hardly stranger danger, but I want to yell "fire!" all the same. "No thanks," I tell Bo. *"Nessa?"* I call to her more forcefully. "You said you'd take me home."

She comes up for air again. Her eyes narrow at me. Mine narrow back.

This is going to be ugly. I'm positive of it.

I wait in the passenger seat of Nessa's car just in front of her apartment building. Her car smells like an ashen campfire from the residue of cigarette smoke, so I prop the door open, hoping the carcinogens inside will flap out like black bats and be replaced with fresh air.

Up above on the second-floor landing of her apartment, Nessa and Cooper kiss each other underneath her porch light. She said she'd keep her promise to take me home, but she's sure taking her sweet time about it, which gives me more time to realize what an ass I was for coming along. A fact that has me festering inside, like the boil on Granddad's foot, which has gotten so bad these past couple of weeks, he's had to wear socks and sandals instead of his favorite brown leather lace-up shoes.

I rudely honk the horn. She pulls away and Cooper

slips back into her apartment, where hopefully poor Bo is rethinking his sideburns. Nessa clomps down the steel stairs, which look like a gigantic xylophone.

Once in the car she says, "You'd better have a brain tumor that needs tending to right now." She's still panting from her make-out session as she starts the car and pulls into the street. "What the hell is wrong with you? You and Bo seemed to be happy."

"You're mad at *me*?" She's out of her head. "I don't appreciate you telling everyone Trevor cheated on me."

"Calm down, Molly. I didn't tell everyone." She reaches into the mouth of her purse for a cigarette as she navigates the dark road ahead with one hand clamped on the wheel. I punch my finger on the button that lowers my window.

"You should have left me alone tonight, Ness."

"Oh." She slaps her forehead in a fit of sarcasm. "That's right! You wanted to crawl into a hole and eat away at your fingernails because of what happened with Trevor. How could I forget?"

"I don't bite my fingernails anymore," I say in my defense, but I curl my blue chipped nails under. "And you don't understand." I close my eyes, lean my head out the window. I just want to get back to the Banshee and away from her.

A few minutes later, Vanessa slides the car next to the curb in front of the closed used-book store a few shops down and across the street from the Banshee. "Happy now?"

"Thrilled," I say. I grab the door handle, ready to lurch.

Nessa takes a deep drag of what's left of her cigarette, its orange tip glowing brighter. "I don't know what's going on with you. Why are you so determined to be a downer lately? What's wrong with having fun?"

"Fun?" I roll my eyes. "Maybe it's fun for you to lick some guy's face, but that's not my definition. If you don't remember, I just broke up with someone. You could at least be more sensitive about it."

Smoke pours out of her mouth. "Sounds to me like you're taking the whole Trevor-cheating-on-you a little too seriously. I mean, Mol, c'mon." She looks me smack-dab in the eye. "You had to see *that* one coming."

Sharp words that jackhammer directly into my stomach. "How can you even say that?" I spit. "That's not true. He and Felicia were broken up."

"For what? A *day*?"

My head becomes like the boiling kettle on the stove at home, hissing with steam. "Are you saying that it's my fault Trevor cheated on me?"

She shrugs. "Trevor has a reputation. You wanted to be with him so badly you overlooked it. And hooking up with anybody is a risk."

"It wasn't a hookup. We were together for *three months*." I push back tears with a dose of rage.

She drops her cigarette into the generic-soda can inside the cup holder. "But he's an ass! Haven't we established that already?" Nessa shakes her head. "The worst part is that you're letting Trevor get the best of you. I mean, why can't you just admit it was a bad call and move on?"

"Move on." I throw up my hands. "Is that why I should be making out with Bo right now? Would you consider that *moving on*?" A tear trickles down to my chin and dangles there. "That's not how I deal with things, Nessa. And I told you that already. I'm not like you. I wish stuff could roll off my shoulders, but it doesn't."

"I'm just trying to help you."

"So, what, you think being at your place tonight and going to the Poseidon last weekend was helping me? Be honest, Ness, you don't care about what I need. I'm here tonight because *you* needed me."

Her face contorts into disgust, her eyes watery and fierce. "I can't believe you just said that, Molly." She reels back, shaking her head. "You know what bothers me the most? How hypocritical you are. You think I'm incapable of listening to you and that I'm selfish, while you totally blew me off to be with that jerk-off Trevor. And now that he's gone, you act like my sole purpose in life is to listen to your despair."

At this moment I feel like we're ripping apart at our already loose seam. I wipe my eyes on the fabric on my shoulder. "You don't understand what it's like because you never let yourself stay with a guy long enough to get attached."

Her breathing is hard, labored. The tears brimming

at the edges of her eyes flit down. "Don't try to make me feel bad about who I am, Molly!"

"God, Ness, at least you *know* who you are!" I yell back.

"If I'm so horrible and toxic to you, then why don't you get out of the car?"

"Fine," I say, pushing myself out the door. I shut it and watch Vanessa turn her tiny car out into the street, through a green light, and away from me.

I slump down on the curb, watch as my tears plip, plop into the gutter. I didn't know it would be so hard to say what I had to say to Nessa.

Normally, when we fight, we wrap it up nicely somehow in the end. I have the urge to call her right now, to take it all back.

Without Vanessa, who do I have? Certainly not Trevor. That's a horrible reason to reach out to her, though, just because I'm scared to be alone.

I get up. Wipe my face briskly with my hands. Up, up, up. I've got to do, act, right now. I jaywalk across the street and step into the Banshee, expecting it to be right where I left it, as if I pressed Pause earlier and now I'm ready to resume playing.

A few things remain the same when I walk from the hallway to the entrance of the pub. "Hey, Molly!" yells Aunt Tip from her position behind the bar. I scan the room and see there's still no sign of Daddy and the uncles, who're obviously pulling a late night, but the businessmen who were here earlier have loosened their neckties.

Evan Truso, whose brown hair looks like a broccoli floret, sits onstage with a harmonica bracket around his neck that resembles orthodontic headgear. With his guitar on his lap, he strums Bob Dylan's "Honey, Just Allow Me One More Chance."

"Molly girl!" Aunt Tipper waves me over to the bar, which I'm supposed to steer clear of after eight. I lace through the tables toward her, still shaky from my episode with Nessa.

"You're back!" she says, and it makes me feel like I've come home.

22

I'm up early Saturday morning for the Girl Corps fund-raiser. The looming event propels me out of my bed and into the bathroom, where I squeeze a squiggle of toothpaste onto the toothbrush bristles and work each tooth until froth drips out my mouth.

I spit and move toward taming the beast of my hair, while staring at my green eyes in the mirror until my entire face is a blur. I had trouble sleeping last night, my fight with Vanessa never quite leaving my thoughts. I don't regret lashing out at her—I feel entitled to my anger—but I do wish she had texted me a small note to let me know bygones were bygones. At least, that's what I think I wish.

I still have a half hour before I have to be next door, so I grab my purple spiral notebook, shoved in the top drawer of my desk amid unsharpened pencils

and a few bubble-gum-colored Pink Pearl erasers. I'll
see Rhondi in a few minutes, and I never followed
up on goal setting. I want to be ready to answer if
she asks.

Girl Journal Entry Three
QUESTION **60**:
**What is one goal you want to achieve in the
next few months?**

I just saw a blurred image of myself in the mirror,
and that's really how I feel, like a blurred portrait. Trevor and Vanessa, two defining lines of
my life, have been smudged, and I have to put
myself into focus, try to define who I am instead
of having others define me. I want to be able to
connect with others in a better way that
doesn't compromise who I am. Like with Vanessa,
I love her, I do. Walking away last night was one of
the hardest things I've ever done, because the
part of her that doesn't listen to me is the one
part that I can't tolerate anymore. I hate that I
have to leave an entire person because of one
part I don't like.

So, my goal is that—how do I word this? I
wish I could connect to people in ways that make
me feel good about who I am instead of always
second-guessing. With Trevor, I always worried
that I wasn't experienced enough. With Ness, I
worry about letting her down, as if a no from me

will lead her to explode. I want to know how to be myself with other people, like the way I am at the Banshee. In a way that people will accept me, instead of expecting something that I probably won't be able to deliver.

During setup in Dede's butter-colored kitchen, Rhondi stands behind the birchwood butcher block. Her jeans look like sausage casings around her thick legs, and her entire torso is ensconced in the red satin of her cape. The girls and I sit around the kitchen table as she commands our attention with her silence, then speaks.

"Girls." She leans her arms against the podium of the butcher block like she's a politician ready to deliver a campaign speech. "Today we pay homage to our founders, Lila and Frances Larson." Her brown eyes glint with pride. "The Larson sisters reaped a bounty from their apple and cherry orchards and donated their profits to the poor. We, girls"—she pauses, as if we're on the cusp of making history—"we will make cherry jam." I'm startled that our project is not apple-related.

The girls murmur and Maribel points to the crates of cherries behind Rhondi. "That explains all the cherries."

There must be five crates stacked on top of each other, cherry stems poking out from the wooden slats like lobster antennae.

"That's right, Maribel. We've got a lot of work ahead of us. Let's get started!" With that, Rhondi points us to our stations. I'm in the Fenway kitchen amid the buzz of high-pitched Girl Corps voices. We have a common goal, which is more than I can say for my relationships with Trevor (who wanted to have sex) and Nessa (who's in search of thrills). Cherry jam is a common goal I can handle.

Hatsuku, Emily, Sophia, and I sit at the kitchen table, each of us with a square of white plastic cutting board. We pound cherries with rubber mallets and extract the pits, flinging the pitted washed cherries into a yellow ceramic bowl centered on the table.

Maribel and Ayisha help Maribel's white-haired grandmother stir the fruits of our labor with sugar and pectin, then boil the thickening mixture over a camping stove set up on the kitchen island.

Dede and Rhondi wield tongs above pots of boiling water on the stove, sterilizing dozens of jars.

"Isn't this great?" Emily asks. She centers a cherry on her board and smashes it with the mallet like she's a lumberjack.

"Yes, it is," I reply. I have surrendered to the fact that the phone in my pocket will not vibrate. My hands are drenched in cherry juice, which seeps beneath my fingernails and drips down my fingers. It's like I'm seven years old again, in the side yard of my house, preparing mud pies. It's nice to have the freedom to make a mess.

Hatsuku's long, perfectly pin-straight hair is tied back and shiny underneath the recessed lighting. "Molly, why are you in Girl Corps?" She whacks a cherry. *Splurt!*

"Because you gals are fun to hang out with, that's why." *Sputt!* "Plus, it's all good, you know? You girls do good things and it makes me feel inspired to do good things, too."

Hatsuku and Emily giggle. I know I shouldn't play favorites, but they're so darned sweet. Then there's Sophia, who hasn't so much as looked up from her cherry pitting.

"So, Sophia." *Whack!* "I like your haircut," I say. Sophia's cut ten inches off her hair and now sports a Dutch-boy style. Her dark brown eyes would probably light up if she dared to smile.

She places a cherry on the board with such precision you'd think she's trying to balance a marble on a golf tee. "I didn't cut it so it would look good," she says under her breath. "It's part of my goal to connect with others. You know"—she stares up at me—"for *charity.*" She says it slowly, as if I don't know the meaning of the word. "I donated it to Locks of Love. Please don't make fun of me." She thumps the mallet on top of its target.

Hatsuku and Emily both flinch at the movement.

I gently place my mallet on the cutting board and reach my stained hand out to Sophia, who looks at my hand, then at me, with surprise. "I wasn't trying to make fun of you, Sophia."

Hatsuku and Emily wait expectantly for Sophia to reply, and it occurs to me that I may have just gone where no other girl has gone before. This little network of girls is no different than the tangle of cliques at Hilldale High School or the not-so-bully-free zone on the playground of an elementary school.

There's always one kid, one girl or one boy, in any situation, who the others avoid out of fear. Looks like Sophia holds that position here.

Except, at the moment, Sophia doesn't appear to be intimidating. She stares at me for another moment, silent, then her chin aims down at her pile of cherries. For a moment I see a young Vanessa, on guard. The type of person who's going to lash out at you first in an attempt to prevent herself from getting hurt. "Sophia," I say. "It was nice of you to give up your hair for a good cause. That's amazing. I just gave up my straight iron last week and thought *that* was a sacrifice."

I continue. "What you did is selfless, Sophia. I don't think I'd ever be compassionate enough to do that."

She hesitates, then nods, and I swear, I see her lips curl ever so slightly. I wouldn't go as so far to say that she's smiling, but it looks like the beginning of one.

"Now"—I line three cherries in a row on my board—"let's show these little fruits what we're made of!"

Whack! Wick! Splat! Feels good to hit something.

Whack! Wick! Splat! My eyes fix on each crushed cherry. They become cracked oysters offering up priceless pearls.

Hatsuku and Emily take my cue and follow my pound-and-splat style of breaking out the pits.

Whack! Wick! Splat! "We're unstoppable!" I say.

Whack! Wick! Splat! "This is awesome!" says Emily.

Sophia smiles and forms a reckless line of cherries, then crushes each one. *Whack! Wick! Splat!*

My heart bursts; warmth fills my chest. "There you go, Sophia! Now we're a force to be reckoned with!" They follow my cue as we increase the output of pitted cherries with our newly adopted style. It feels good to do something right and have the support of these girls. I'm so used to following that it's a new sensation within me to lead. Like I've just discovered a third ear or an eleventh finger. "Let's keep going, girls!"

"Excuse me." Rhondi's finger firmly taps my shoulder, which halts our cherry-hammer rhythm section. Hatsuku, Emily, and Sophia freeze mid-whack.

Rhondi stares down at me. "Um, can I speak with you for a moment?"

"Did you see our method here, Rhondi?" I can't contain my excitement. "Look how fast we're pitting these."

"Yeah!" says Hatsuku. "The bowl's almost full."

"That's great." She gives Hatsuku a nod. "Molly, I need to speak with you."

"Is something wrong?" I ask. I'm confused as to what I may have done to piss her off. The girls gaze up at her with curiosity.

"Please," she says, her red lips pursed.

I'm annoyed that she has the nerve to be impatient with me. I've just increased cherry production and made the smile-less Sophia smile.

"Okay," I say, perhaps with too much sarcasm in my tone. I wipe my stained hands on a paper towel, scoot my chair out from the table, and follow Rhondi into the entry hall, where she dwarfs the huge spray of dried flowers on a decorative table behind her.

Rhondi crosses her arms over her watermelon-sized shelf of a chest and taps her foot, in what looks like an orthopedic white shoe found on the likes of a dental hygienist. The sound of the tapping drowns out the voices that echo from the kitchen.

"You're pounding those cherries beyond smith-ereens."

"Wait, I'm confused," I say. "Aren't we supposed to be smashing cherries?"

"Certainly, but you seem like you're taking some-thing out on them—"

I cut in. "We were having fun." I cross my arms over my chest, too, defensive. "I didn't know they weren't allowed to have fun."

The foot stops tapping, but I'm still caught in her severe gaze, like this is a me-versus-her tournament. "I don't appreciate your tone." She loosens her arms and her glare softens. "Are you upset about something?" She looks concerned, and she waits for my answer, her eye-brows raised in anticipation. She really wants to know.

"No, it's not that at all."

"We need to be on the same page. I want the girls to be surrounded by positive morale."

"*Morale?*" It slips out. "We're jarring jam, Rhondi, not fighting a war."

She shifts her weight, gives me another once-over, and walks closer to me, her orthopedic shoes squeaking against the tile. If I was off the hook before, I'm now squirming on it again.

"Did you see Sophia?" I say fast. "She smiled, Rhondi. Isn't that a good thing?"

"It's not just about fun and games, Molly. It's important that these girls have serious role models."

"I guess I don't understand how being serious all the time is a good thing." I'm saying what I want to say; right or wrong, it's honest.

"We have a lot coming up in the next few weeks." She counts off on her fingers. "Next week alone is the jam sale, our annual backyard campout, and a hike in Mount Laguna. If you're going to be with us, I need to know you have self-control, that I can trust you to lead."

"You think I can lead?" I can barely say no to a horny boy or refuse a backstage pass to the Poseidon. I stand up straighter, as if there's a thread being tugged inside my chest. "I can lead," I say, almost more for myself than Rhondi.

"It's important, Molly. I don't want these girls to get the idea that the events themselves are meaningless. There's a *reason* behind everything we do. And I see them getting attached to you. I don't want that to happen if you're just here for kicks." This is very mama bear of her. My stomach twinges because I don't have my mama bear standing over me, protecting me.

"I want to be here, Rhondi. Really, I wouldn't be here if that weren't true." I assume that's what she wants to hear, and it's what I want to say. "You said yourself that actions speak louder than words. I'm here. I'm writing in the journal."

"I was in the Corps when I was your age. People made fun of me. You've got to have a backbone to stand up to that kind of scrutiny."

I gaze up at her. "I'm working on that, Rhondi. Just know I wouldn't do anything that would hurt the feelings of these girls. I'm not going to walk away from them."

"Let's see you follow through, then." She looks beyond me toward the kitchen. "Right now, we need to get in there and get back on track. You're on stove duty."

I'm not sure whether this is a demotion or a promotion, but I take it. For the rest of the afternoon, Rhondi leads the girls in song while we work. They're songs that I've heard before, but ones I never quite got to memorize or bother to sing myself.

I don't. Sing along, that is. Nope. Not one "Miss Mary Mack," "Sipping Soda from a Straw," or "On Top of Spaghetti" escapes my lips. Maybe I'm trying to prove to Rhondi—and to myself—that I'm serious about this, too.

But after the jars are labeled—MADE WITH ♥ BY GIRL CORPS—and I walk across the Fenways' lawn three hours later all alone, I catch myself. Whistling. I'm in Girl Corps now, and I chose it. It's my decision. I own it!

It's a realization that makes me run onto our dead grass and spin into a cartwheel.

Vanessa doesn't bother to call me Saturday night. Neither does Trevor. And that's fine, because why would I expect them to call? It's just weird—and pathetic—that the absence of two people can actually strangle my social life. How did my world get so small?

I can do things to connect with the outside world. At least, that's what I tell myself.

So I head over to the Banshee with my men for karaoke night and even help Daryl in the kitchen with the preparation of mulligan stew. My fingers get sore from peeling and chopping a ten-pound bag of russet potatoes.

After listening to a few sets of karaoke, I slink back into Aunt Tip's office, where I plop on the couch with my spiral-bound Girl Journal and the *Girl Corps Handbook*.

There's a whole process of goal setting that I didn't

know existed. In Girl Corps, G.O.A.L. is an acronym. *G* is for *Goal,* as in setting a goal. *O* is for *Organize,* setting out steps you will take to reach the goal. *A* is for *Act,* actually going through the steps you planned, and *L* is for *Looking Glass,* seeing yourself achieving the goal, looking ahead.

I'm not sure I can remember all this, but it makes sense somehow. It's almost reassuring to know that if you just follow these four steps, you can reach your desired goal. I just have to figure out what exactly it is I want.

Daddy pops his head in while I begin to spin my pen along an empty page, trying to get it to release ink. From the stage, the screech of a woman's voice belts out "R-E-S-P-E-C-T, find out what it means to me!" Daddy squints his eyes and, using his better judgment, shuts the door behind him.

"What's going on, Mol? Don't have the ears for karaoke tonight?"

"Not really."

"What you writing there?"

"This?" I flap the flimsy notebook. "It's a Girl Journal. For Girl Corps."

He nods, the wisps of his fine hair moving like Christmas tree tinsel. "I think it's great that you're involved with that lately. I mean, you didn't ever seem interested as a kid, so I, you know, never pushed you. With your mam, it might have been different. She was always one to encourage me to step out of my box, as she called it."

"How so?"

"Ah, well, take Agnes Flynn, right? She's always had

that Irish dancing here on Monday night. She got me to try that."

I laugh. "No, not you?"

"Sure indeedy. Wasn't any good, but your mam knew how to nudge." He puts his hand on my knee and gives me a squeeze. "You know, if it weren't for her, I would probably have never left Ireland."

"I thought she came because you wanted to come."

"Oh no. I wasn't as creative as she was. I couldn't imagine living in a different place. But she"—he points straight ahead—"she could see the details. The palm trees, the warm sandy beaches we have here. Yep, she knew how to make you believe."

I slide closer to him on the couch and rest my head on his shoulder. "I wish she were here."

"Me too, girl." He looks at me with glossy eyes. "Me too."

Sunday morning I write my first "action steps" entry in my Girl Journal, which is supposed to help me "bring my goal to life." Then I finish up my "In My Own Words" synopsis of act 1, scenes 1 and 2 of Shakespeare's *Twelfth Night*.

Basically, a duke's in love with a woman he hardly knows, and another young woman pretends to be a man so she can get a job with the lovestruck duke because she needs work, but the woman the duke's in love with falls for the guy who's really a girl pretending to be a dude.

I thought my life was confusing.

Someone knocks. "Come in."

I fully expect it to be Claire, given the softness of the sound, but Vanessa walks through the door and I feel my blood drain from my face, like I've just seen a ghost.

She's newly showered, her long hair straightened and reaching down the middle of her back. She flings her purse on the floor like she usually does. The comfort of old habits shakes me inside, like we never had an argument the other night, like she never heard me say that I need time alone.

"Hey, Mol." She plunks on my bed, leaning back to let her strong, brown arms support her. "Thought you might want to make peace over pancakes at the Hotcake House."

I didn't ask for peace, but I don't want war, either. "I thought we were, you know, gonna take a break."

She shrugs. "We've had arguments before. Nothing a little pancakes and syrup couldn't fix." I gotta hand it to the girl, she's resilient. Me, I still feel guarded and unsure.

She looks down at my open spiral Girl Journal next to her on the bed. Oh crap.

"What's this?" She twists over to read it.

"It's mine." I leap out of my chair and lunge for it, but Nessa's already got it gripped in her hands. She stands up on my bed with her shoes on and shows no consideration for my clean comforter or my privacy. She scans the lines of writing in the notebook.

"That's personal, Vanessa. It's not for you to read." She presses her palm outward, her face wrinkling into disgust. She looks up at me from my open notebook.

"Nessa!" I scream. "Stop!"

"This is brilliant, Molly." Her sarcasm edges near anger. " 'Girl Journal Entry Four,' " she reads in a theatrical voice, " 'Goal Setting'!" It's the entry I wrote this morning.

I stand on the bed now and face her, but she doesn't relent. She keeps going, reading this morning's Girl Journal entry word for word. " 'G is for goal! State your goal: I want to be a stronger person.' "

I leap forward to grab it from her hand but she jumps down from the bed and I break my fall against the headboard.

" 'O is for organize!' " She steps onto my desk chair now, the loose leg causing it to teeter.

"Vanessa, I mean it!"

" 'Organize your goal into a clear statement: I want to feel better about myself because most of the time I feel like crap and would like to stop feeling like crap as soon as possible.' "

"Vanessa!" I jump down from the bed, leap up, and grab her arm, squeeze it. "Those are my personal thoughts. Give it back!" Tears start spilling down my face. I hate how she does this to me!

She forcefully pulls her arm from my grasp. " 'A is for action steps! Make two action steps to reach your goal and the core values it will require. Number one: I will stop letting *Vanessa* order me around. Core Value at work: Opinion. I will need to use my voice and conviction to tell her when I'm uncomfortable with her plans.'"

This time I go for it. With both hands I reach for her arm and wrestle her off the chair. "What are you doing?" She loses her footing and tumbles down, but she clenches her hand around the notebook until we're both on the wooden floor.

She holds it away from me, reaching high so that even though we're both on the ground, I have to break her strong hold in order to grip it. I don't stop, though. I clench down along her arm like I'm climbing a rope, one hand over the other on the muscle of her arm until I grip the bottom rung of the metal spiral.

We tug-o'-war until it rips, me getting the smaller half of the wishbone, Nessa claiming the notebook itself.

Our quickened breathing fills the air. Her face is purple, streaked with tears. "Screw this," she says, and flings the journal across the room and stands up, while I try to do the same. "I can't believe you actually have to write goals to ward me off. And Girl Corps? What are you? Six years old?"

"It makes me feel good, Nessa, which is a lot more than I can say for this friendship." I sniff, wipe my face against my inner arm.

"You want distance, Molly?" She reaches down to grab her purse from the floor, not bothering to wipe her own wet face. "You got it."

She opens the door and slams it behind her.

Aunt Tip is always telling Clem to be careful what you wish for. "Argh!" I yell.

I know exactly what Aunt Tip means. I meant what I wrote, and it felt easy writing it down. Hearing what I wrote in Vanessa's voice made it sound so harsh. I want to run down the steps after her and apologize for hurting her feelings. But I have feelings at stake here, too. My apology would only deny what I wrote in my journal. I trust that what I wrote was true. It's just the truth coming out in a way I could never say to her face, and maybe that's the only way it could ever be said.

I reach down and pick up the severed pieces of my notebook, unravel the pages that Nessa ripped out. The edges are jagged but the writing is still there. I open my desk drawer for tape. I don't care if it's ripped. I'm not going to throw this away. No, I've come too far to turn back now.

24

On Monday morning, I hitch a ride with Daddy and the uncles, even though it's 6:45 a.m., a solid thirty minutes earlier than I normally leave with Vanessa. It takes me a half hour to walk, so it's still worth the extra sleep in my eyes to get up.

The weather stays truer to fall than summer now. There's actually a little nip in the air. The palms along the street sway in the hint of a breeze. I walk toward the dumpy work truck and take shotgun next to Daddy, while my three uncles sit in the back of the cab. The truck smells like a collision of men's toiletries. Spice. Mint. Musk. With a hint of polyurethane.

"Vanessa sick today?"

"Nah," I say. "We're just not seeing eye to eye right now. I think we just need a little break." I haven't mentioned my falling-out with Nessa to Daddy. I've gone over it so much in my head that I don't want to hash over it all again.

"Nothing wrong with that," Daddy says. "Everyone needs a breather once in a while."

Daddy cranes his neck, reverses down the driveway, and shifts back into forward gear. A moat of stubble surrounds his mouth. "Are you growing a beard?" I ask.

He rubs his chin. "What, you don't like it?"

"No, actually, I think it'll look good on you."

Uncle Garrett leans in from the backseat, the ringlets of his black hair still glistening, not having dried yet from his morning shower. "What about that boy Trevor, eh? Haven't seen him around much this past week." He chuckles. "Did we scare him off with our little lecture?"

I look over to Daddy, a little stung that he didn't mention the Trevor breakup to his brothers. I'm forced to tell my uncles. "We broke up."

Uncle Rourke sighs. "That what's been bothering you?"

"Yeah," I say.

Uncle Murph reaches to pat my shoulder, the bald bulb of his head shining. "You're better off without him. You don't need nobody who's gonna trample all over your heart. Nothing's worth that, and certainly not love."

"Now, now, Murph. Don't be so callous," Uncle Rourke chimes in with his soft voice. "Better to have loved and lost than never to have loved at all."

"Eck!" says Uncle Murph, like he's spitting out a rotten bite of meat. "That's a bog o' crap, Rourke, and you know it. Look at Garrett here—his ex would've eaten his heart in one gulp." He uses his chubby hand to illustrate a movable jaw. "Instead she gnawed away at it. Was that worth the lovin'?"

"That was bad judgment on my part, Murph," says Uncle Garrett, a tinge of hurt in his eyes. "Don't go telling the girl that love don't matter." He taps me on the shoulder. "I'm with Rourke on this one. Nothing ventured, nothing gained, Mol."

" 'Sright," says Uncle Rourke. "You can't put a wide head on young shoulders. Molly's got to go through it. We all go through it. You live, you love, you lose. But eventually, you gain a little wisdom about it all."

"And," adds Uncle Garrett, "there are as many good fish in the sea as ever came out of it. You hang in there, girl, the right fella will come along. Someone who's gonna respect you."

This is beginning to feel like a "best of" worst love clichés ever.

"Feelings don't mean nothing!" shouts Uncle Murph. "Dr. Love Lynnette on the radio would tell you that herself. We can't be run by our *feelings* or it all goes to hell."

We pause at a stop sign in front of a house whose owners have gone all out on Halloween decorations—from Styrofoam tombstones to a dozen scattered jack-o'-lanterns. Halloween's this Sunday. My spandex unitard hangs useless in my closet because I won't be going to Zach's Halloween party on Friday.

It's a night now reserved for the Girl Corps backyard campout.

Daddy stays stopped at the sign. "That's not it, Murph. You've got this thing about love all wrong."

"Then enlighten us, Owen," Uncle Murph says, inviting a comeback.

Daddy peers back at the uncles. "None of you fools ever had the courage to get married. To be with *one* person, through thick and through thin. If you had, you'd know love." He gazes out the windshield.

Then he looks at me with his eyes blue and bright. "If I'd given up the first time I had a broken heart, I'da never met your mam, Mol. Like I told you before, you got to take the risk. It's worth it when it works, so you don't go letting some bad experience with someone define what it's all about. You're gonna hit dead ends sometimes, but you keep on until you meet the right one." He puts his foot on the gas and pulls away from our prolonged stop.

No one contradicts him, which is rare in this family. Someone's always staking the claim to the last word. We're all quiet for the remaining blocks and I let what he says steep. I've never thought of Trevor as a dead end; instead, I see him as a huge wall with something on the other side. The thought of breaking through that wall seems insurmountable, but if it's a dead end, it's like what Rhondi said, getting back on

track, which means turning around and finding another path.

When we turn into the cul-de-sac near school, I
don't attempt to get out of the car until Daddy locks
eyes with me. "Thanks," I say to him. "I like what you
said, Daddy. Makes me feel like there's actually a light
at the end of the tunnel."

"Of course there is, Mol. If there weren't, you
wouldn't be livin'." He leans over and kisses my cheek.

I turn to the backseat, to my trio of hulking uncles.
"Bye."

"Keep your head up, girl!" says Uncle Rourke,
climbing into the front after I jump out. Once he's set-
tled, the truck sputters away.

I wait in the parking lot until 7:20, which I now
realize was a stupid move on my part. I have to pass
Vanessa, who hangs out at the mouth of the parking lot
with Jasmine Mendenhall and Callie Drucker.

I nervously twitch while considering my options. I
could walk through the parking lot toward the football
field to avoid Vanessa—I've got the time—but the reality is I'm going to see her again and again and can't put
off the inevitable. Still, there's plenty of time to face
that, so I trot in the opposite direction and step
through the wet dew of the field.

During lunch, I stay inside the safe haven of the
underground PE locker room amid the lingering smell
of body odor and the fruity spray that's squirted to
cover it up. Sure, there are other people I could hang out

with, but that would require me to reach out, energy that I just don't have at the moment. For now, I'm happy in the sensory deprivation tank of the locker room.

When I enter ceramics at the end of the day, Ms. Pinkwater and Trevor are spreading our completed projects out on tables. He smiles at Ms. Pinkwater, allowing me to catch sight of his dimple, and a spear strikes my stomach. The first look at him each day is always the hardest; it's just best to redirect myself.

My glazed foot turned out pretty well. It's shiny and the toes aren't to scale—the pinky toe looks like a shrunken corn kernel—but it's my piece of art.

A sheet of blank paper sits next to each project. An electric current runs through my veins at the sight of Trevor, but it's just lust short-circuiting my resolve. I need to follow through, to turn around and walk away from what I know is a dead end.

All of us are asked to stand at the edges of the room, and when the bell rings Ms. Pinkwater waves her arms. "Today, we'll take a gallery walk. Each person will write a comment on the paper next to the project." She turns to pace in the other direction, and the hem of her ankle-length skirt spins like a hula hoop. "Be honest," she says, "and encouraging. Artists need to know what they're doing right, too. That's how we flourish."

The entire class moves like a broken merry-go-round the rest of the period. Projects range from simple—bowls with experimental patches of glaze—to more complex—attempted Lord of the Rings figurines. There's one project that is a blob, an artistically challenged piece that only contributes to making me feel better about myself. At least I got beyond the hunk of turd-looking clay and made a foot.

Toward the end of class, Ms. Pinkwater tings her bowl. "All projects need to go on table five for me to grade." We shuffle toward our own projects. "Take your peer critique, and please make sure you take the time to read the comments. You'll grow from the honest feedback. Tomorrow, you'll have time to think through your next project with that feedback in mind."

I grab my paper and, like the fool I am, scan down to where I find Trevor's recognizable all-caps penmanship. His is clearly the biggest chunk of writing.

MOLLY, YOUR SCULPTURE IS ORIGINAL (LIKE YOU). FUN (LIKE YOU). DIFFERENT (LIKE YOU). I HOPE YOU SEE IT THAT WAY, TOO. YOU'RE ALWAYS HARD ON YOURSELF, BUT THIS IS SIMPLE AND DOESN'T CONFUSE THE ON-LOOKER. IN FACT, IT MAKES THE VIEWER REALIZE THE BEAUTY OF SIMPLICITY. IT IS WHAT IT IS, BUT IN A WAY THAT IS SIMPLE AND BEAUTIFUL (LIKE YOU).

I can't look up at him because if I do, I might throw myself at him. I have to remember that they're just words, not a love sonnet. I glance over the other comments (*Funky foot!*), but my eyes quickly return to Trevor's paragraph.

I'm on an emotional teeter-totter, but I've got to keep my head on straight. Lead myself out of this one little step at a time.

I think he's looking at me—I see the outline of him next to Ms. Pinkwater, but I don't dare confirm. I fold my feedback sheet in half, walk to my messenger bag, tuck the paper inside, zip the bag. Small movements, but they consume time, prevent me from slipping up.

By the time Wednesday night arrives, I'm excited about the Girl Corps jam sale—it's my first big social event of the week and the first time since Saturday that I've seen the girls.

Dede and Claire wait in the black SUV as I run out of the house toward them. I take the empty space in the passenger seat as a nice gesture and strap in.

"Where's your cape, Molly?"

Dede bites her lip. I turn to Claire in the backseat. "You know, I forgot it." It's true, but it covers up the bigger truth, which is I'm not prepared to wear the cape in public. Thankfully, Dede's already pulled onto the street so I don't have to run back into the house and grab it.

Dede drops Claire and me off at the storefront of Kino's Organic Marketplace, which used to be an

Albertsons supermarket but closed after a bigger and more super supermarket was built a few blocks away in North Hilldale. Uncle Murph gets our produce at Kino's but refuses to buy meat here because, in his words, "You can't find a piece of meat that's got any fat on it in the place!"

The girls set up outside the store, where barrels and bins of produce are on exhibit, a big display of pumpkins tumbling over blocks of hay. Our table sits next to a giant barrel of Red Delicious apples (1 LB FOR $1! the neon yellow sign reads).

Rhondi bends over a foldout table, her cape swishes to the side, and thus the general public can see her big blue-jeaned bottom as she pulls down the last of four table legs. There's already one table set up, and it's decorated with doilies, jam, and picture frames holding photos of the Girl Corps planting seeds or group-hugging in a fill-in-the-blank location.

When Claire and I approach, Rhondi's already got the other table assembled, and the girls stack jars of cherry jam on it from boxes. "Okay, then," she says when she sees Claire and me. "We're all here! Who's ready to sell some jam?"

I'm delegated to be banker and sit at a small table next to a rack of plastic potted herbs ($5!). I do my best in the first half hour of the jam sale to count and recount money, because the girls are hard-core sales-people. "Homemade cherry jam for sale!" "Help Girl Corps help others!" They practically accost shoppers entering the market with the jars of jam so no one can resist.

But later, the fizz dies down. Maribel and Hatsuku lean against the apple bin like jaded jam salesgirls; Sophia, Emily, and Claire still work the entrance, where the pumpkins upstage them.

When an elderly woman accidentally drops a bag of groceries in the parking lot, Rhondi says, "Molly? Watch the girls for a moment, please?"

She rushes out to the lot and starts collecting cans and lemons from around the elderly woman's feet.

I step away from the money table and corral the girls near a bucket of yellow squash stippled with barnacle-like blemishes (4 FOR $1!). They're dragging and need a little fun.

"You want to sell more jam?" I ask.

"Of course," says Sophia, who holds two jars of jam up in the air.

"Let's show these people they *need* the jam, then." I face away from them and, in my loudest Banshee voice, say, "What do you want?"

The girls look at me, confused. I stage-whisper, "Jam."

"Jam!" they yell.

"When do you want it?"

Confusion again, so I offer another stage whisper, "Now!"

And we're set. "What do you want?"

"Jam!"

"When do you want it?"

"Now!"

We may sound like a protest march, but people stop to listen. Ayisha, Sophia, and Claire approach customers while the rest of us chant.

Rhondi rushes back from the parking lot. "Girls!"

I smile at her because of the enthusiasm we've sparked. "What do you want?"

"Jam!"

"When do you want it?"

"Girls!" Rhondi booms. "We are not here to cause a racket." She throws me a wicked stare. "Let's get back to selling jam the way we were doing it before."

Again, just when we're having fun, Rhondi feels the need to see something wrong with it, with me.

Toward the end of our night, the last fifteen jars of jam remain on the table. Rhondi pep-talks us in a manner that might make you think we'd been swigging Gatorade and wiping the sweat from our brows. She must assume it's fine when she rallies them, but when I do it, it's a crime.

"Look," she says, "we can't give up now. We've got fifteen more jars, six dollars apiece. We can do this."

"Ninety dollars," Sophia says.

Rhondi points at her. "Yes! Ninety dollars more to add to the many we've made today to contribute to the *fund*. Half will go to the charity we choose, the other half toward end-of-the-year activities. This will make it possible. Don't give up."

In the spirit of jam selling, we don't give up. I stay planted in my folding chair, and having read the labels of the potted herbs next to me, I know that I'm enjoying the aroma of basil and rosemary. Rhondi has taken all the big bills and leans over the doily table. She wants to compare units sold with cash at hand. I am happily doing my part at my table by recounting coins when I hear a voice.

"Molly?" A male voice. A *Trevor* voice.

Trevor has just walked out of Kino's and stands here. It's the same Trevor who cheated on me with Felicia Mitchell, and the same Trevor who wrote me the kindest feedback about me and my ceramic foot: *DIFFERENT (LIKE YOU), BEAUTIFUL (LIKE YOU).* He's packaged perfectly in his favorite orange T-shirt, the bronze of his summer tan still aglow. He holds a small paper bag in his hand. How in the world did I not see him walk into Kino's earlier?

He catches me as I continue sliding dimes into a collapsed pile with my finger. "What are you doing here?" he asks.

"Neighbor." My tongue is in a knot and I stop counting dimes. "I'm helping my neighbor." He holds up the little bag; crescents of gray clay remain lodged under his fingernails, a reminder of part of the day we share. Or used to share. I've been so busy SCAB-ing during class because of him that I've barely been able to pay attention to him.

"I had to get lactose-free cream. My dad's making my mom crème brûlée tonight for their anniversary. They're actually staying home, if you can believe it."

Sophia interrupts. "Who are you?" She walks up as close as she can get to Trevor and actually sniffs him.

Trevor leans down to Sophia's four-foot-something frame. I wouldn't get that close to her, but I guess he doesn't know she's probably capable of biting. "I'm Trevor. Are you Molly's neighbor?"

"No." Sophia keeps staring at him. "Are you Molly's boyfriend?"

Oh God, no. Please.

Trevor smiles and the dimple appears. I swear I hear trumpets as it enters the scene. "Do *you* have a boyfriend?"

"I'm *nine*," Sophia delivers deadpan.

"Good point," Trevor says, going with it.

The pattering of Girl Corps footsteps comes over to us. "Hi!" they say, greeting him. They create a human moat around him, for which I'm thankful. It protects me from the urge I always get around Trevor, the one where I want to hurl my body toward his and accept his former apologies.

"Well, hi there, girls," he says, having to move his arms upward because he's got no room at his sides. Except for Sophia, the rest of them are smitten with Hottie-Pants Schultz here. Hatsuku's wide face gleams with joy, and Claire looks like one of those bobble-head dolls, nodding for no apparent reason. Maribel flashes jam jars in his face, and Emily stands close to him without bothering to smile, just staring.

He's got them under his spell. I stand up from

behind the table, but they don't notice. "We should let Trevor get going," I say. The sooner he's out of here, the sooner we can focus.

"You want to buy some homemade jam?" asks Maribel, hiking a jar up closer to his face.

"Of course," he says. I sigh, annoyed that he's prolonging his stay with us. I don't care about his money; it'd be more generous to leave us here without the entrapment of his charms.

Maribel beams, *her* dimples now puckering in full form. He has to step back to make room, then secures the paper bag under his arm and reaches into his pocket for his brown wallet, which looks like a dried-out hamburger patty. He pulls out what appears to be all of his cash. "How many jars can I get with this?"

There's a pause to do the math. Okay. This is kind of him. I see those words on the paper again: *YOU'RE SO HARD ON YOURSELF.*

Ayisha answers. "Eight!"

He hands the bills to me. "Go ahead and put this in the cash box, Ayisha," I say. The girls walk back to my table and put the cash in the box. Then they rush over to get Trevor's eight jars of jam.

"They're fun, eh?" he says, like he's tapped into their secret.

"Yeah." I nod. *Now go away!* I want to scream. *They're my girls and I hate that when I look at you I get weak.* But I'm not crumbling or flinging myself at him. I'm standing. I'm leading myself through this.

The girls approach with Trevor's jam.

"This is perfect," he says, "because I *love* jam."

"No you don't," I say, with surprise. "You always have honey on toast. You told me you hate jam." I'm sure I sound delirious, but for once, I'm not scared of what I have to say to Trevor. I remember what the *O* in *CORE* stands for and any ounce of fear that lay within me vanishes. "You told me you loved me. And that was a lie, too, wasn't it?"

The girls look at him, then me.

"No, that wasn't a lie." I don't believe him. "Girls, can you please give me a minute?"

My emotions are making my heart clench and my hands tremble. I know I should be SCAB-ing right now, but I can't. Trevor watches the girls walk back to the jam table because it's a good way to avoid me.

His arms are loaded down with jars of jam. "I told you I was sorry, Molly. It's not too late, either. Why don't you come to Zach's party on Friday? We could go together." *BEAUTIFUL (LIKE YOU), DIFFERENT (LIKE YOU).*

I want to believe that Trevor is a good boy. That he's not lying about lactose-free crème brûlée. That while his dad blowtorches custard, Trevor will head down the hallway to his room, brush his teeth, comb his hair to the side, get into his flannel pajama bottoms, and climb into his bed to watch reruns of *Jimmy Neutron,* while in the dining room his parents clink glasses of champagne.

But I know that's the part of me that has no bones, the girl inside me who doesn't know who she is and is worried about never finding another person again. That voice is there, but that doesn't mean it's me. "No thanks. I'm not interested." I'm connecting to the girl inside me who has some self-respect, who follows through.

"Molly!" Rhondi shouts. We stand near my accountant's table, away from the rest of the girls, who're in final-sales mode. She approaches and Trevor's eyes widen more.

"You left the cash box open." She squints at Trevor.

"Thanks for the jam," he says to me, suddenly anxious to leave, thanks to Rhondi. "Let me know if you change your mind." God, why can't he just make it easier for me and take no for an answer? I don't say anything and watch him walk across the parking lot toward his dad's navy Lexus.

"Why would you walk away from your resonsibility?" Rhondi snaps.

"I was distracted, okay? I'm sorry."

"That's the point, Molly," she scolds.

She needs to SCAB. The tofu-eating shoppers here at Kino's hardly fit the criminal profile. "I highly doubt anyone would steal from us anyway."

"It's not acceptable." She turns back to check on the status of the girls, who are huddled around a woman who has a toy poodle in her shopping cart. She stands in what I know now to be a disappointed stance, hands on hips, lips pursed. I see it every time I'm with her, which means it must be me.

"The point, Molly, is to stay focused on the task at hand. With the backyard campout this weekend, and the hike, I want to count on you to help lead the girls. You can't get distracted on the trail. They could get hurt."

God, this lady is relentless! And it annoys me that she thinks I'm some kind of slacker. Haven't I proven myself yet? I want to tell her off, but before I can even plot my attack, we get ambushed by a pack of little girls.

"We did it!" Ayisha squeals as she and the rest of the group shout and run toward us.

"We sold all the jam!" says Claire.

"That's excellent, girls." Rhondi now focuses her attention on them. "You did a great job tonight." Rhondi looks each girl in the eye, but not me this time. "You should be proud."

I'm not nominating her for woman of the year, but it's clear that she protects these girls. I'm not one of them, and I always seem to do something that makes her mad, so I'm not sure if I'm ever going to earn her respect. Still, she cares about the girls, and for that reason I can't hate her entirely.

My phone rings. Of course, there was no reason to silence it because it didn't dawn on me that someone would call. Rhondi's attention aims back at me. She crosses her arms and squishes her lips together, expecting me to answer. It becomes a test.

I stand tall, pretend I don't even hear it, although it trembles in my pocket like a jumping bean.

It's Trevor. I know this because even though I didn't answer right away, I do eventually check. Of course, I had to wait till we disassembled jam headquarters.

I even restrained myself as we piled into Rhondi's white iceberg of a van and shuttled over to Denny's for hot fudge sundaes. It wasn't until our minimum-wage-earning host escorted us to our mongo brown vinyl booth that Rhondi excused herself to use the restroom. I mean, at least that's proof that she's human. I was beginning to have my doubts.

It's when the girls and I slide into the booth that I flip out my phone—little beacon of light.

"Who're you calling?" asks Claire.

I wave her off. "I'm just checking something."

"Are you IM-ing?" Hatsuku asks.

"Shh, give me a second."

No voice mail.

Trevor's callback number and text: I'M NOT GIVING UP.

Sometimes there are those texts in your head that you compose, the ones that are long and strong and spell out exactly what it is you want to say. The kind I never write myself. If I could, I would say: FINE,

DON'T GIVE UP, JUST DON'T EXPECT ME TO GIVE IN! The reality is I want to give in, but I already know that. It's old news that I have to put behind me, in my closet with the unworn spandex jumpsuit and the prospect of gliding into Zach's party with Trevor at my side.

"Molly?" I look down at Maribel, who sits on one side of me and whispers up into my ear. The rest of the girls go unseen behind the huge menus. "How many calories in a slice of banana cream pie?"

Oh. Ohhh. "Miss Maribel?" I ask back. "Does it really matter?"

Her eyes are so big and brown and innocent it kills me to think there's even a twinge of self-consciousness in this girl. "You're beautiful," I say. "If you're hungry for pie, eat pie, hon."

She smiles. I dab her nose with my pointer finger. "Come to think of it, I'm hungry for pie, too." As if anything is more important than this right now. I slip my phone in my pocket.

Rhondi comes back to the table and blows us all out of the water; she orders the Grand Slam breakfast, an act that in and of itself warrants some admiration. Our food arrives and I stab my apple pie à la mode with a vengeance.

"Now." Rhondi twiddles her napkin in the creases of her heart-shaped mouth, then digs into her carpet-bag. "We've just a few things to discuss since there won't be a meeting tomorrow night."

She distributes a handout. "This is our schedule for the backyard sleepover—"

"It's at my house this year!" Claire blurts out.

"Yes, Claire. And I'm expecting you girls to sleep. Especially because the hike this year will be a bit longer." She reaches back into her amorphous purse and extracts a pair of reading glasses with bright orange frames, then slides them on. They make her look older, and I can't seem to gauge how old she might be. Forty-five? Fifty?

"Now." Rhondi peers through the half-moon lenses. "We'll spend the night at Claire's. Use the checklist so you know what to bring. Then, Saturday morning, we'll leave at five sharp for the hour drive to Mount Laguna."

"Wow," I say, more as a reflex than a statement. All eyes on me. Rhondi's peek out from above her glasses. "I just—it's early is all. Are we leaving that early for a reason?"

"Yes, Molly. We're going to Mount Laguna to walk along the Pacific Crest Trail. If you've read the handbook, you know that the Larson sisters strongly urge us to experience nature—"

"I know," I interrupt. "Their first hike was in Walla Walla, Washington." I strike back at her, disappointed that I need to prove myself, but also knowing that she challenges me with that sometimes condescending tone of hers.

Rhondi nods. "It's going to be a long day and we'll

need to get back to the van by sundown. That's why we need to leave early. So we'll have our tent campout at Claire's Friday night. Arrive by six, please."

Uh-oh. I raise my hand again. Rhondi eyes me with annoyance. "Yes?"

"I'm playing with my family's band Friday night. I can't make it till ten or so."

"You mean you're not coming to the campout?" whines Ayisha.

"I'll come, but later. I have a previous obligation." Rhondi looks perturbed. "An obligation to my *family*. I play the accordion and I need to *follow through* with that commitment."

"You play the accordion?" says Sophia. "I play the flute."

"That's great, Sophia. Maybe you can bring it Friday night. I'd love to hear you play."

"Since it's going to be late when you get there, we may want to save that for another meeting," Rhondi says, and I see Sophia's shoulders sag a few notches.

"It's not like it would take a long time, Rhondi," I argue.

"Let's just stay on schedule, shall we?" she says. "Sophia"—she turns to the girl—"I'd like to hear you play, too. I just think it would be best when we don't have so much on our plate, okay?"

Sophia accepts, and I realize that Rhondi is trying to make Sophia feel better, so I don't press the issue.

"So then, Molly, you'll be there around ten. We'll

expect you." Wow. She's actually giving me some slack. This may work after all, because for the first time, I get the feeling that Rhondi is going to need my help on that nature hike. Why else would she let me arrive four hours late?

I do something stupid Thursday night. I tried to resist the spandex unitard, but I can't help it. Daddy knocks on my door after I've done the deed. "Mol?"

"Yeah?" I freeze in front of the mirror.

"Can I come in for a sec?"

Given how tight this spandex suit is, I doubt I could wriggle out of it quickly. "Sure, come on in."

Daddy halts when he sees me. "What's that?"

"It's a bodysuit."

"You're not wearing it anywhere, right?" There's worry in his eyes.

"No, not anymore."

"Whew," he sighs. "That's good."

I sit down in my desk chair, the spandex squeezing my body like a too-tight sleeve. "You wanted to talk to me?"

Daddy sits on my bed in blue jeans and short sleeves, his after-work costume. "Wanted to check in with you. Your uncles and I are leaving early tomorrow for Palmdale. Weekend job. We'll be home Sunday. You got all you need for that hike?"

"Yep."

"You leave when?"

"Saturday. Crack of dawn. I'm spending the night at Claire's tomorrow, though."

"You sure you can do Battle of the Bands tomorrow night with your granddad?"

"I was planning on it. I'm fifteen, remember? I don't need sleep."

Daddy laughs. "Good. With Clem visiting his brother in LA, I know your granddad will love to have you onstage with him."

"We'll rock the house."

He looks at the sculpture of my mom perched on the nightstand, and when he reaches over to hold it, it shrinks, appearing smaller and more delicate in his big hand. "I remember when I made this."

"How long did it take you?"

"Oh"—he looks up to the ceiling—"a few days, maybe. She's all I could think about, and I think carving this kept me from going crazy, like I always did." He replaces Mom on the nightstand, careful that she doesn't wobble. "It's a good thing, to stay busy. Productive."

"I wish I didn't have to think about that so much. It'd be easier if focus came naturally."

"Well, whether it's natural don't matter. Point is, you're practicing." I believe that. No one ever tells you when you're learning to read and write that being human takes practice, too. I just might need more practice than the average homo sapiens.

Daddy stands up from the bed and kisses me on the

forehead, then tousles my hair. "You have fun this weekend. Your granddad will take you to school tomorrow."

"Sounds good." I stand and give him a hug.

He squeezes me tightly. "You're making your own
way, Mol."

"Yeah." I nod when he pulls away. "I'm trying."

"No." He shakes his head. "You *are,* girl."

26

During ceramics class on Friday, Trevor spends most of his time at the sink, rinsing plastic buckets and sponges for Ms. Pinkwater.

Ms. Pinkwater sits at my side for a few minutes to coach me on a different glaze technique for the coil vase I completed in a record two days. "It's drip glazing, Molly," she says, holding the *p* at the end of *drip* so that her mouth makes a popping sound.

I follow her instructions and dip the vase upside down in a thin, matte glaze, then double-dip into an umber glaze, halfway so that the vase looks like it's got a flame scorching down to its base. "I like this," I say.

"It's a nice piece, Molly." She smiles. "You can put it in the kiln," she says with the satisfaction of a teacher who's just taught something.

Trevor's still at the sink, so I take my time in the

empty kiln and find a place for my vase on a lower shelf, toward the back. It's neat in here, a pre-gallery of pieces: bowls, plates, pinched pots, and figurines.

"That's a cool vase you made." I turn to face Trevor, who stands behind me in the kiln. He crosses a hand over one shoulder to scratch his neck.

He must have been here a few seconds if he saw my vase, because now it's tucked away. My lips feel tight, my heart races, but I force it. "Thanks."

My hands rub the residue from the chalky shelf on my work shirt. Trevor tilts his head. He's let his hair grow a bit instead of keeping it trimmed, like he normally does. It looks good, but I think he'd even look good bald, Uncle Murph style.

"So, you're not gonna go to Zach's with me?" Trevor asks.

"I'm playing at the Banshee tonight."

"What about after?"

He's been trying for two weeks. I keep saying no, and I'll never know if he's serious about me if I keep saying no. That's not me talking, though. That's the scared part of me who wants to hang on. I would think that each "no" would be easier, but I push it out like a woman in labor: "No."

"We've got to start somewhere, Molly." It's almost worse that there's no dimple right now to distract me. "How about a ride home, then?"

I stop again. *We*, he just said we: *We've got to start somewhere.* Suddenly it's more than *me*. I've managed to forget there's a *we* in this equation. There's Trevor, who I'm having a hard time ignoring, and me, who I'm having a hard time controlling; then there's this separate *we* that hasn't had the chance to repair itself because I'm so busy with the ignoring and controlling. I don't squeak out an answer, so Trevor does it for me.

"So we can walk to the parking lot together after school," he says matter-of-factly. I have my chance to correct him and put up a protest here, but instead I rush past him into the classroom.

Later the bell rings, signaling the end of the day. And before I can even look to see where Trevor is positioned in the classroom, I grab my messenger bag and run, run, run into the air-conditioned ice cap of the math/science building next door. I break through the chain of people walking toward their lockers and slide into the girls' bathroom and into a stall. For the next twenty minutes, I crouch on the toilet seat and breathe heavily. I realize how close I was to buckling under Trevor's persistence.

I know I should feel proud of my escape, but I don't. I'm not convinced running away is all that courageous. It just lets me avoid having to confront Trevor.

Early Friday evening, I focus on my campout checklist. I grab an ancient musty sleeping bag from Daddy's organized closet. I've also snagged the Jacob's digestives—an Irish biscuit—for my nonperishable snack, a PowerBar, and a bottle of water. Next: warm socks. Rhondi said the two main sources of losing heat are through our feet and head, and we'll probably be cold in the morning portion of the hike. I'll need to borrow a hat from Daddy, but I'm set in the sock department. Wall-to-wall hardwood floors get cold, even in mild Southern California winters.

When I reach down into my bottom dresser drawer for my socks, there, rumpled and wrinkled, is the red capelet Claire and Dede gave me a few weeks ago. At the time it just seemed silly, but I wonder why Rhondi hasn't even demanded that I wear it to the meetings. The others wear theirs. Does she not think I'm worthy?

Shaking it out, I let the silky fabric cover my hands, then whisk it across my shoulders and tie it in place.

In the mirror, I look like what I am: a fifteen-year-old girl wearing a Girl Corps cape. But the cape does give me a feeling of power. Like in sixth grade when Vanessa and I slipped on her mom's high heels and I felt an instantaneous taste of womanhood.

Except it's backward this time. I'm a fifteen-year-old trying to get a glimpse of the child she can't really remember being. Or I'm a person pretending to have superhuman strength.

The truly strong wouldn't think twice about Trevor and his invitation to Zach's party. The truly strong would have forgotten the nice words he wrote on my feedback sheet: *BEAUTIFUL (LIKE YOU)*. The truly strong wouldn't have to talk herself into being strong.

In honor of All Hallows' Eve, I've paired my cape with
the navy spandex and slipped on my black swim-skirt
to cover my lower-body contours (or lack thereof), and
worn them with my black leather thrift store boots. The
effect is bizarre, but not altogether wrong. After all, it's
a costume.

"I feel like I got ABBA in the car with me," says
Granddad as we drive toward the Banshee.

I eye him in his leprechaun outfit, which he normally reserves for St. Paddy's Day. "And you're looking
quite realistic yourself. If I didn't know any better, I'd
think you might be hiding gold under your hat." The
white fuzz of his long sideburns and the fluff from his
hair are a perfect touch beneath his velvety green cap.

"I tell you, we're certain to be the most colorful
band this evening."

"Thanks for dressing up with me, Granddad." He agreed to dress up tonight even though the Banshee's official costume party is Sunday, on Halloween.

"You think you're ready to play tonight?"

"Why wouldn't I be?" I straighten out the cape under the strap of my seat belt.

"You never practice at home. You're always leaving Buttons at the Banshee."

He's right. I can't remember the last time I actually brought Buttons home with me. "I haven't had the time."

"And you never will," he says. "Time doesn't just exist." He raises his hand; a gold cuff link holds his shirt sleeve together. "You *make* the time."

"Well"—I lean over and pat him on the knee—"isn't that what I'm doing now?"

"Yes, love." His furry eyebrow dips as he winks. " 'Tis."

Ten acts have signed up for the Battle of the Bands at the Banshee.

Granddad and I share a booth and devour our bangers and beans while Agnes Flynn pounds her drum to a fast version of the normally solemn "My Bonny Boy." The night wanes. Malcolm Gallagher plays a song I don't recognize on his bagpipes, but the result is a fit of terrible coughing at the end of his set that sounds like a musical performance all on its own. Hoots ups the ante with his lively spoon instrumental of "Dirty Old Town;" my right arm becomes the target of his crescendo.

At nine-thirty, Granddad and I mount the stage. He knows my time constraint, because he or Aunt Tip has to drive me home so I can make it in time for the sleepover at ten. But we have time to do our thing, so I'm not worried.

Granddad and his flute along with me and Buttons roar with a version of "Spanish Lady." Each time Granddad pauses with the flute, I stream in with Buttons, pumping faster as we reach the end of the song. I prolong a G chord, then Granddad flits in with his flute. The crowd hollers and we're showered with applause that proclaims us the victors.

"Molly!" Aunt Tipper reaches up to the stage with a cool, damp bar towel.

Never again will I perform in spandex. It doesn't breathe, and the leather of my boots doesn't make me any cooler. "Thanks," I say. I reach down for the cool towel and wipe my face.

Granddad leans over to me in his costume. "What would you like as our grand finale, Mol?"

The clock reads 9:40. We can make it. I throw the towel on a stool and start pumping out a D-C-D chord progression and Granddad shouts, "Step It Out, Mary!"

The song is fast, upbeat, and brings a swarm of enthusiastic dancers to the dance floor.

But in the middle of Granddad's solo and right before my own, I notice an eye-patched Trevor, which causes Buttons to slacken in my hands.

I recover and look out at Trevor beyond the small

bright lights above me. He stands next to a table where a middle-aged couple cuddles up, tapping their feet in time. Trevor's T-shirt is ripped and it looks like he smeared a black beard on his face with coal.

I can't believe he turned up here, especially since I blew him off after school.

Trevor smiles at me and then moves his gaze to Granddad on flute, whose feet jig in the quickened last sixteen counts of the song because I haven't joined in to finish it myself.

The small crowd doesn't mind my mental fart and bursts into applause, Trevor included. I'm frozen on-stage.

"Excellent job, Molly B!" Granddad says, bringing me out of paralysis and into a hug. He bows and gets his applause, then waves over to me. I curtsy to more applause and a whistle from Trevor.

I turn and tuck Buttons away in his case with the hope that when I turn back around, Trevor will be gone.

Except he's not, he's right here, at the edge of the stage. I step down. "That was amazing." Trevor makes a fist. "You crank on that accordion, Molly."

"Great job, girl!" yells Hoots, who gives me a thumbs-up from a few feet away.

"Thanks," I say with a wave.

"That was terrific, Molly," Malcolm the bagpiper adds. "You're tough competition, but 'twas a good one."

Trevor steps closer to me. "You're like a celebrity

here." A song roars out of the speakers unexpectedly and causes Trevor to flinch. Aunt Tipper's got the sound system back on since we're finished with the live entertainment. Trevor starts to say something, but all I can hear is the Clancy Brothers singing "All for Me Grog."

I point to my ears and yell, "I can't hear you." It's probably for the better, too. I've got ten minutes to get to Claire's house.

We weave through the crowd, and I take us down the hall, into Aunt Tipper's office. I close the door behind us and waste no time. "I have to be somewhere in ten minutes."

Trevor scans the room for the first time, his eyes following the vertical panels of wood near the sofa. I cross my arms over my spandex chest. He focuses on me.

"This is for you." From his plastic sword sheath he extracts a long-stemmed orange rose, the bud protected by a cellophane sleeve. Inside is a small white card, but the writing faces the other way. He holds it closer to me.

If I take it, it will loosen my resolve. I know from watching television that flowers can have that power on women.

He offers it again. "It's orange."

"I see that," I say.

"The florist said it's a mix between a red rose and a yellow rose. Passion and friendship. Like our relationship. Us." He's using those pretty words again. *BEAU-TIFUL (LIKE YOU).*

SCAB! CORE! GOAL! I call upon the sorcery of the acronyms, but I'm stuck, the letters tumbling upon each other like a broken alphabet.

"Molly, what's wrong?"

"We don't have a relationship, Trevor." As I say it, my eyes go blurry with tears.

"We do, Mol. That's why I'm here." He steps forward with the rose and takes my hand in his free one. "Come with me tonight. We'll have fun and hang out just like we used to do. You've just got to give me another chance."

"I told you, I have somewhere else I have to be." I close my eyes, count to ten, but the emotions are still there. Fiery, like the inside of the kiln when it's baking.

"You've got to—"

"Stop." My hand squeezes his and I use my other hand to form a cup around his. "I keep thinking maybe you're right, you know? But you're not. We're not together. You ended it when you cheated on me, because I just couldn't keep up with you and you got impatient."

"I'm so sorry, Molly." He slowly wriggles his hand free of mine and reaches out to touch my cheek. "I miss hanging out with you."

With eyes closed, I lean into the curve of his hand. "Trevor." It comes out as a whisper. It's happening. I know this is wrong, yet I feel myself loosen, from my neck to my elbows to my knees.

"I was stupid." He's closer now, his nose brushes

the tip of mine. He's making it so easy for me. I could crawl back into this with him. "How many more times do I have to tell you that I want to be with you?"

"Please don't do this." He's so close I feel the supple outline of his lips graze mine as I say it.

"You know you want this, Mol."

My body shudders and my eyes unlock. The moment pops like a bubble. "Don't tell me what I want." I take a step back, then another. Trevor becomes smaller with each step. "You think you can cruise in here and make me second-guess myself." I've spent the last two weeks with the girls, the journal, Rhondi—I feel clear with them, stronger. Not like this. I sniff. "But I won't let you, Trevor." I wipe my eyes with my spandex sleeve, walk toward the door, and open it for him. "Please, go."

He starts to say something but I cut in. "Leave, Trevor."

He raises his palms in protest. "But we were just—"

"Leave!" I scream.

He sets the rose on the sofa and I close my eyes while he walks by me and out the door. I shut it behind him, lock it in case he should change his mind, and lean against it until my body slides down. I slouch into a ball.

I just followed through. But I don't feel great. My stomach hurts, my head throbs, and the tears burst out. I run over and bury my face in the scratchy couch and scream, but someone knocks on the door.

"Molly? You in there?" It's Granddad.

"Yeah."

"Shouldn't we be going, love? It's after ten."

Hell-damn-crap! I grab the rose and move so fast toward the door that my cape flutters behind me.

By the time Granddad drops me off in front of Dede's house, it's almost ten-thirty. Rhondi's white megavan is parked in the driveway.

I sprint directly over to the Fenway house without going to mine first to retrieve my bag. I've brought the rose, figuring I can give it to Dede since she's the only flower lover I know.

I knock on the door, hoping that I won't get too much flak from Rhondi and the rest of the night will run smoothly. I wait a few moments until Dede answers, but she opens the door only halfway and offers only a half smile.

"Hi, Dede." My voice is still shaky from Trevor. "I know I'm late, I got caught up at the Banshee." She hears something behind her and looks, then nods to someone I can't see who's inside the house. Dede steps back and Rhondi squeezes herself out the slice of doorway and onto the porch. She looks like Rocky Balboa in matching gray sweatpants and sweatshirt.

"I'm sorry I'm late," I say. "I had to rush over here, but I can explain."

She shakes her head in dismay. "I knew this was all a joke to you."

"What do you mean, a joke?" She can't be serious. "I'm here."

"Yes, but following through is more than just showing up, Molly."

"Let me apologize to the girls, please." Deep breath, she can't kick me out now. "It'll be fine."

"Dede and I have spent the last twenty minutes explaining to the girls what may have caused you to not show up. So, what? You come in, it's all fine, and then next week, it's something else? I told you, they're attached and I'm not going to let them get hurt just because you don't know how to keep a commitment."

"You can't do this, Rhondi."

"It's not fair to the girls."

"You know what I think?" I tremble.

"I'm not interested."

"You're afraid that your little order of girls will spin out of control if—God forbid—they see someone make a mistake. And have you noticed that every time I have fun with them, you butt in and stop it? You're threatened by me, aren't you?"

"You, young lady, are out of line."

"Then tell me, what is it that I do that has you constantly riding my ass?"

"Molly?" Claire, Ayisha, Emily, Maribel, and Sophia peer out from the front door.

Maribel asks me in a hushed tone, "Why are you yelling at Rhondi?"

"Girls," says Dede, pulling them back, "stay inside."
She shuts the door.

"You're out." Rhondi's tone is flat, stone cold.
"Don't come back." She walks toward the door and
opens it.

"You can't do this!" Tears stream down my face. I
stomp my boot. "I've been a part of this."

Rhondi turns. "Not anymore." And she closes the
door firmly behind her.

I storm up the steps to my house, but I don't have my keys. No way to get inside. I doubt picking the lock with the rose stem would work, and it's all I've got. Dammit!

I pace the porch. I've tried to be a better person through my actions, but for what? For this? Now I have nothing. No Vanessa. I hold up the rose. No Trevor.

Inside the plastic shield the unread white card fits snugly against the rosebud. I reach my fingers inside and pinch it out: I LOVE YOU, MOLLY. It's enough to push me over the edge. And it does.

I know there's not a chance in hell you'd find anyone from Hilldale High School riding a bike to a party, but I also know it's the quickest way for me to get to Zach's. Besides, the thrill of the wind against my face fuels me, makes me feel wild, like I do inside. I've been contained these last few weeks, thinking I'm better off with the continuity of the Girl Corps.

For what? To get kicked out?

I huff up Marlborough Hill, past Trevor's house, where there's no Jeep in his driveway. I keep telling myself I'm not going to Zach's for Trevor. No, I'm going for me, despite what I know is right or wrong. I want to be wanted right now, by people my own age, not sulking at home, alone, where I know I'll just talk myself into feeling better or write in my journal.

I stop short of Zach's house when I notice Trevor's Jeep, parked a few houses down and across the street. Even though I told myself I wasn't here for him, my heart flutters knowing he's here.

I park my bike two doors down, in someone's driveway behind their parked RV, where no one can take it, should they want a rusted Huffy cruiser.

Eleven is still early in party terms. A few unknowns hang out in front on the porch step, guzzling from orange cups, and a bass beat pounds from inside the house.

A guy who wears a Superman T-shirt says, "Hey, who're you supposed to be?"

For a moment it's a profound question, but then I remember it's Halloween and I'm wearing spandex and a cape. "A superhero."

"Which one?" he asks. He looks sincerely confused.

"The generic one." I approach the door, gently

twist the knob, as if I'm trying not to wake anyone inside, and glimpse a mass of people gyrating to Lil Wayne (or is it Rick Ross? I can't keep them straight). It's packed inside, though one would never know it from the outside. In order to get across the room into what might be the kitchen, I squeeze through a swarm of people and get caught in a hip thrust from behind, which actually helps me move forward.

The house is lazily decorated with nothing but fake spiderwebs, which aren't pulled properly, so it looks like everything is covered in clumps of cotton balls.

In the kitchen I see Zach, the football type, his buzz haircut grown out a bit from Hell Week a month ago—the football players shaved their heads out of either drunkenness or unity. "Beer bong!" Zach yells. His T-shirt reads: THIS IS MY HALLOWEEN COSTUME.

I don't go over to say hello; it would just draw attention to the fact that I came here alone, a fact that's starting to make me feel self-conscious. I could have stayed *home* and felt alone. If I keep moving, it'll look like I'm purposely walking either away from or toward something, which is not far from the truth.

I pass the dining room table, where a cluster of upperclassmen plunk quarters into cups, and then step through a side door to the backyard, where an even larger infestation of people congregates. I stand on a step and scan the yard, but no Trevor. I don't even see Nessa.

As I look out over the crowd I notice duplicate

costumes: girls with devil horns or bumblebee antennae headbands, guys bespectacled in oversized pimp
sunglasses or crowned in cowboy hats. Trevor's pirate
hat would stand out if he were here, but there's no sign
of it. Where could he be? My curiosity leads me down a
few steps outside and through a maze of people toward
the side of the house, where I discover trash cans, next
to which a guy and girl lean against the stucco wall of
the house and make out.

Suddenly, I'm knocked to the ground, my knees
sinking into the damp grass as I land. "Man! I'm so
sorry. I didn't even see you." The wet earth seeps
through my spandex, drenching the entire front portion of my body. I'm a fool, facedown in the lawn. At
least I'm off to the side of the house and not in clear
view of everyone, but for some reason, it makes me feel
more alone, because at least if I were with someone, we
could laugh about it. Instead, I'm a girl who came here
alone and fell alone and feels alone.

The guy who bumped me has taken his sweet time,
but he bends down, cradles my elbow, and pulls me up.
Swirls of water stains blot my front. The guy, buzz-
haired and thus a football player, pinches his face. "I'm
so sorry."

"It's fine." I hold my arms out to my side. "I don't
care." And I don't. Tar and feather me, I deserve it for
coming here in the first place.

"Here." He offers me an orange plastic cup with
what looks like punch in it.

The throng of people murmurs around me, sounding like background chatter at the Banshee. I'm going to have to walk back through them to leave, but with the stains and grass flecks in my hair, in won't be as easy to be invisible. I grab the offering from Buzz Cut, tilt my head, and guzzle. The cold fruity liquid tickles my throat.

"Whoa," says Buzz Cut. "That's a hell of a glug you got there."

Although there's a harsh aftertaste, my mouth is parched, so I continue to drink. Glug. Glug. Glug.

A burp escapes, the rekindled flame of bangers and beans trailing behind it.

"Right on," says Buzz Cut, flipping me a thumbs-up. Nice to know that after all these years of primping in the morning, all I really needed to do was burp to get a guy's approval.

"Thanks," I say, as if he did me a favor. Moments later, my head feels light, my stomach full, and my eyes still wander the outside for a sign of Trevor.

I head back into the house, most of which I haven't explored yet. Back at the quarters table, the same players vie for a shot at putting a quarter into the cup. "Molly?"

Vanessa leans against the back of a dining room chair, a new fixture from the last scene. She plays spectator to the game at the table.

"What are you doing here?" Jasmine stands next to Nessa. She wears a short black skirt, a V-neck, and a witch hat. I'm relieved that she doesn't have on the spandex that Nessa and I wear. Silly as it sounds, I would have been jealous had Vanessa allowed someone in on our spandex plan.

"I just was looking for someone."

"Who?" asks Nessa, narrowing her eyes at me, suddenly back inside my business.

"*Someone.*" This is too awkward. She knows I'm here alone. Who else would I be with?

"Are you drunk?" asks Jasmine.

"No."

Jasmine laughs. "It looks like someone spilled a keg on you."

I look down at my wet front as if the drenched spandex against my skin isn't enough confirmation.

"You're looking for Trevor, aren't you?" It's a question, but it sounds more like an accusation. Nessa shakes her head in pity at me.

I can't take it, so I turn and leave, but when I wriggle through into the front room, near the entryway, sitting on a chair, is a pirate. It's the same pirate who stood in the crowd at the Banshee a few hours ago. The same one who scrawled I LOVE YOU on a florist's card. I can't figure out why he'd try so hard when right now, there's a nurse on his lap. It's not even a Felicia nurse. It's a brown-haired one, a girl I don't recognize. Both of them bob in and out of a kiss, their heads swaying, his hand cupping her bare knee.

The tears burst through, down my face, my chin. I want to scream, but I can't. The past few weeks Trevor has tried to convince me that we should be together. And somehow I knew deep inside—not even that deep, really—I knew this would happen eventually. Not with another girl, but with Felicia. Still, what does it matter? It's not me.

I curl my arm up to wipe my eyes. I should be thankful that I'm standing here, hidden in the gyrating crowd, watching Trevor and this girl make out, because it's just more evidence that he's a liar and I'm merely a conquest. That someone can say anything—*I'm sorry, I love you*—and that it can mean absolutely nothing. But I'm not feeling gratitude at the moment. I only want to disappear.

I'm not sure where to go. I step backward instead of forward, though. If I want to leave, I have to pass Trevor and the girl and that would be too much, like walking through fire.

So I keep backing away, past Vanessa at the table, past a cluster of people near the back door, and outside, where I run to my corner, by the side of the house, near the make-out couple. An orange cup sits on the air-conditioner vent. I grab it and glug down the punch. Glug. Glug. Glug.

I think it's my third. No, it's my fourth. The make-out couple are actually nice people. They come sit down next to me on the ground. We giggle because it's wet, but they sit down anyway. "Why are you crying?" the girl from the couple asks.

"I cry too much." I tell them about Trevor.

I tilt another swig and shake my head. "What's that word—you know when you mess things up for yourself and then it can't get worse so you keep going?"

"Self-mutilation?" asks Pilar. She's the girl of the couple and her costume is her work uniform: an apron wrapped at her small waist that says DENNY'S on it. I told her I ate pie there two days ago.

"No. Like, okay." I blink hard to clear my head. "It's like, like—I totally can't stop saying 'like.' But anyway—I came here by myself to see Trevor and knew I shouldn't, but did anyway? What's the word, you guys?"

"Dude," says Phil, the boy of the couple. He wears a paper Krispy Kreme hat but doesn't work there. He got it when he bought a donut. "That's called love."

"No!" I point at him. "I'm looking for that word. Like when you make things worse for yourself?"

"Stupid?" asks Pilar.

"No, no." I wave my hand. "It's like to wreck yourself."

"Oh!" shouts Phil. "Masochistic."

"Sort of, but you keep coming back for more pain."

"That, Molly," says Pilar, pointing at me, "is sabotage."

"Yes!" I yell, and take a drink, but the cup is empty. "That's it." I burp. The sky slopes when I look up at it, like the earth wears a crooked hat. "I don't feel so good."

"You gonna puke?" asks Phil.

"Maybe?" Bangers and beans churn in my stomach.

"Stand up, Phil!" yells Pilar. "Let's get her to the bathroom."

Phil and Pilar help me up, and they are good friends. I feel like my feet are wheels! But I don't feel good. "Bangers and Beans." The more I move, the less I feel.

"What?" one of them says. They sound the same now, slow-motion-talking like.

They lead me into the house. "Coming through!" says Phil.

"Molly?" Nessa's there now, too.

"She's gonna barf," says Phil. Or Pilar. Maybe it's me, I don't know.

The other people around me blur, like a page in a Where's Waldo? book. I love those books, but the thought of all of those bodies and finding Waldo in his striped shirt causes my head to spin faster.

They pass a line of people outside the bathroom. "I'm sorry," I say. "I'll be s'quick." Hands help me inside, where I droop over a cold bowl.

"It's okay," says Vanessa. "I got her."

A door slams. "Here, lean into this." I have to close my eyes now because it's all spinning. My head droops down low and heavy, my neck as flexible as Buttons.

My stomach heaves. Then a cyclone. "G'night."

29

It smells like Victoria's Secret Love Spell body spray. My gag reflex kicks in and a sour taste fills my mouth.

There are ten bricks on top of my head and I wonder if I've been buried alive. But I open an eye, the other one burrowing into a pillow. I'm on a bed. The sting of my dry contact bites and I wince. I blink to moisten it, then scan the dusky room: A Razor Hurley poster of Karl the Drummer striking an X with his drumsticks. To the left of that, an open laptop, the hard drive humming. Farther left, a silver wall hook draped with necklaces that look as colorful as a Mardi Gras parade. Down and on the bed next to me a blanket of brown hair: Nessa. All clues that I'm in Nessa's room.

I close my eye, this time in shame. I can't even remember what happened last night. I mean, I remember Trevor and the girl. Yes, I remember that part, but I don't even remember getting here, to Nessa's house.

I inch up my neck, which makes my head swell, and flicker my other glued-up eye open. The clock reads 6:30.

The girls and Rhondi probably just pulled into the Mount Laguna visitors center. I missed the campout and because of that, I threw away everything that went with it. I didn't even try to follow through, did I? I mean, sure, Rhondi's a hard-ass, but I should have gone home and showed up this morning, standing next to the van, ready to leave.

I turn to look again at Nessa, a hump under her purple comforter. She must have helped me last night, for which I'm thankful. Even though we had a falling-out, she was there. I guess just because we've gone in different directions doesn't mean our paths won't continue to cross.

The slight movement of my head makes me dizzy. I reach over and shake Vanessa's shoulder, which peeks out from her white tank.

"Nessa?"

"Urgh." She moans.

"Ness?"

She twists her body and stretches her arm in the air. Her hair catches under her shoulder as she turns to face me. I always thought she looked her best in the morning, without makeup, her face au naturel, her brown eyes softer than when she globs on the thick black eyeliner.

"How did I get here?"

"Man." She waves her hand over her face. "That's some breath you got on you."

"C'mon. What happened?"

"Well." She props herself up on her elbow and rubs her eyes. Yawns. "You really want to know?"

I slap my forehead with my hand. "Was it that bad?"

"I followed the two people who brought you in the house. You puked in the toilet." I vaguely remember that, but the image of the line of people stands in my memory. "Then you passed out. Right on the bathroom rug."

"My God, did everyone see?"

"No, the door was shut. I did text Jasmine to come into the bathroom with Bo so they could help me get you out of there."

"Oh no." I shake my head. Ouch. "I don't remember anything."

I gently drop my head back into the downy puff of Nessa's pillow. "What a disaster."

"Nah." Nessa waves this away. "I wouldn't worry about it. We did a good job of walking you out of the party and into my car. It was getting you up the steps of the apartment here that was hellish."

"I can't believe that I was such a freaking basket case."

"Don't be so dramatic, Mol."

I moan. "I saw Trevor making out with some girl."

Nessa looks down and pulls a thread from her comforter. "You okay?"

"Yeah. He just hasn't stopped trying to mend fences." I tell her about Trevor coming to the Banshee. "I totally refused to go with him to Zach's. But then I got kicked out of the Girl Corps and instead of trying to mend that fence, I lost my mind."

"You got kicked out of Girl Corps?" Vanessa suddenly looks up in surprise. "What, did you burn their flag or something?"

I tell her about arriving late at the sleepover.

"Well," says Nessa, "not that you should care what I think, but it sounds like you could mend *that* fence, given the fact that those little girls probably idolize you. Plus, everyone makes mistakes, right? You're only human. Rhondi's got to understand that."

She's right. I didn't follow through, and that was my bad, but I don't think I admitted that. I got so caught up in being defensive, I never acknowledged the fact that I had control over being late. "Ness?"

"Huh?"

"Did it ever occur to you that I wrote that stuff down in the Girl Journal because it was too hard to say to you in person?"

She blows a spout of air upward, causing some baby hairs along her forehead to wave. "No, I didn't think that, Mol. I guess because I *say* what I think, no matter what. You know that."

"I try to do that, too, but you don't listen."

"I just saved you from drowning in a pool of your own vomit last night. Please don't tell me I'm a crappy friend."

"You're not, but it's just hard to get through to you sometimes."

She nods and fingers the satin ribbon along the edge of her bedsheet. "Right, but you gotta love it or leave it. It's who I am. Good or bad, you know?"

At least she's got the guts to admit it. "Well, it means a lot to me that you helped me out last night, Ness, even though we haven't been around each other much lately."

"I'm not some psycho harpy from hell, Mol. I wouldn't have left you there to suffer." She reaches out and gives me a playful shove. "No matter what, me love you," she grunts.

"Me love you, too." We may not have a perfect friendship, but at least we can see that and admit what we need, which is more than I can say for how I felt a few weeks ago, when I was too scared to speak up. What's happened to change that, I'm not exactly sure. Is it this whole whirlwind with Trevor? Or could it be the Girl Corps? The Girl Corps, which I'm no longer allowed to be a part of.

The fact that Rhondi booted me out last night causes a new pang in my stomach that joins the throbs and nausea of my hungover head. But maybe Vanessa's right about something: I can at least try to mend the damage I've done with the Girl Corps.

I can't reverse time, but I think I have an idea of how I can move forward.

"Hey, Ness, what time do you have to be at work?"

"Nine. Why?"

"I have a huge favor to ask you."

30

Heavy metal Puddingfuss serenades us on the stereo as the landscape on the freeway becomes browner. The wonder of living in Southern California is that you're an hour away from everything: the beach, the desert, the mountains.

My head's a murky slosh pit. It doesn't feel better when I close my eyes, but it doesn't feel good with them open. It's mental torture.

About forty minutes later, I have to pop my ears again for the tenth time. Nessa stopped by my house so I could get my supplies and do a quick change into shorts and a T-shirt, but I kept the cape around my shoulders.

I point to the sign that reads MOUNT LAGUNA, CLEVE-LAND NATIONAL FOREST NEXT EXIT. "How is this a forest?" asks Vanessa. "It's so dry and brown."

"I don't know. Maybe that's what I'm gonna learn today."

"So, why are you so serious about this, Molly?"

We exit the freeway and follow the arrow that points left onto an ascending curvy road. "I can't explain it. I mean, the girls, they're sweet. They make me feel good." Vanessa peers over at me. "Don't even say it, Ness."

"No," she says in an easy-breezy voice. "What could I possibly say that you didn't jot down in that journal of yours?"

"I told you. I was just thinking things through."

"All right. Fair enough."

"It's obvious that no matter what, we're here for each other, right?"

"Must be why I'm driving your sorry ass up a mountain."

And that's it. Puddingfuss continues to sing, and Nessa and I drive, surrounded by the beige and olive green trees that seem to be getting greener as we climb up and up in the little blue car that could.

At the Mount Laguna campground, we loop through a circle until I spot it. "There!" Rhondi's *Titanic*-sized van is parked in a spot next to a brick building that houses a bathroom.

"Okeydokey, then."

"Sure you don't want to come along?"

"Can't blow off work today."

We look at each other. Nessa's dark features and that voice inside her are so strong. "Ness, thank you."

"You'd do the same for me." She's right. Nessa looks out her window, craning her neck at the tall pines above. "Now scoot, I gotta fly down that hill so I can make it to work on time."

I grab my backpack from between my feet, lean against the door to open it, and then wave as Nessa reverses and loops back toward the entrance.

It's chilly up here. A different climate that feels good against the burbling of my head. I'm still dizzy, but a breath of wind passes through the tall trees with a whisper, grazing my body like a gentle remedy. I don't have a plan. I'm here to follow through with what's in my heart and my head, that's my answer. The question is, where are they?

Prepared in sneakers, I pull my hat from my backpack and find the sign that says PACIFIC CREST TRAIL. The arrows point in both directions. To the right, west, the trail goes up, up, up. But to the east, it looks even, following the curve of the side of the hill. I know Rhondi's a diehard safety nut so I go east, hoping that I don't fall off a cliff and get eaten by buzzards.

There's no trail of crumbs to guide me, but the path itself is worn and smooth. The sun creeps higher in the sky, following the imaginary curve of a rainbow. It's beautiful out here. Daddy talks about missing the quiet of Ireland, and although it's a completely different world there, of water and rain, I think I understand what he means. It's the kind of quiet that fills you, makes you wonder if this is true peace, walking among the crackle of twigs beneath your feet and the twitter of a random bird. The prickle of brush scrapes against my ankles, but I'm just amazed at how so many plants can coexist.

I keep to a quick clip, knowing that it's only a matter of time before I meet up with them. Rhondi can't kick me out of Girl Corps. I know this now. My feet are here, my mind is here. This is where I want to be and I keep moving up the trail.

After forty-five minutes, I perch on a big rock and open my backpack for a bottle of water. I wonder if the trail on the west side was only rough in the beginning, unlike this trail, which seems to be building in its intensity. At least, that's how it feels. It's narrow and there's actually a bit of a ledge.

My head starts to pound again, reminding me of my hangover. I might even be on the wrong path here. What if I judged it wrong? I could reverse, go back and try the other trail. I might still be able to catch up to them.

If only there were other people coming from the other direction, so I could ask if they've seen a gaggle of girls. But it's strangely desolate here. I have a feeling I'm on the right track, though. I check the time on my phone; I'll give it fifteen more minutes. The water refreshes me and I keep walking, remembering the pitch of the other trail, worrying more and more that I've taken the wrong one. Yet this path is steady, hardly the

Swiss Alps, so I'm still thinking Rhondi would've chosen this direction.

Then I hear something.

Voices.

I break into a sprint. Dirt crunches beneath my feet, the water in my backpack sloshes, and when I curve around the next corner, my girls are there, all in red capes. Relief washes over me and my eyes glaze at the sight of them clustered together. But I don't see Rhondi just yet, which is weird. How could I miss her? And there's no sign of Dede or another adult.

"Hey!" I yell out. "You guys! Wait for me!"

"Molly!" screams Claire. "Come quick!"

She's panicked so I race over and it's confirmed, there's no Rhondi. I swallow. "What's going on? Why are you alone?" I can't even imagine why Rhondi would abandon them.

"Oh, Molly, she's dead!" cries Maribel.

"What?" I say. Oh my God. Dead? No, she can't be!

Claire runs and hugs me. Sophia looks up from the beak of her visor cap. "Rhondi fell, Molly." There's panic in her voice. "She's down there."

Down there?

I peek over the edge of the trail and Rhondi is indeed *down there,* faceup, her big red cape sprawled out beneath her. Her eyes are closed. She looks like she's just taking a nap. But her left leg is at an odd angle to the rest of her body. That, plus she's at least seven feet down, on a ledge. If she had fallen several feet earlier, she would've missed the ledge altogether and dropped another twenty feet. Oh my God.

"What do we do?" cries Maribel, her face pink with sunburn, the tears carving through a layer of dust along her face. "We know we shouldn't try and move her, but we don't know what to do."

All five girls crowd close around me now. This is no time for me to panic. I have to be calm here.

I can't believe Rhondi came here alone, without another adult. It seems so unlike her to make a mistake like this, but maybe she's too confident to foresee that something could actually happen to her. Or maybe she really trusted that my presence would have been enough backup for her, which proves that I overlooked the fact that she does have some trust in me.

I get down on one knee to be at eye level and pull out my cell phone from my backpack and dial 911. There's no dial tone, so I hang up. "I need to know when this happened and what happened."

"I don't know. It happened so fast." Ayisha, who's normally confident, hunches over in fear. The others start talking all at once. Still no dial tone on the cell. No signal.

I close my phone. *Stay calm. Stop.* "Whoa, slow down. I just need one person to explain."

Sophia raises her hand. A bottle of water hangs from a lanyard around her neck.

"Go ahead, Sophia."

"It happened maybe thirty minutes ago?" Sophia says. "We were following her and then Rhondi started breathing funny and tripped and fell down there."

"Okay," I say, a bit relieved to know that she fell and might not be dead after all. "First of all, I understand that this is scary for all of us. But we're going to stay calm and get through this."

"But I don't understand how," sobs Hatsuku. She shakes her head and tugs at the rim of her light blue baseball hat. "I don't want Rhondi to die."

I hold my hand to her chin, lift it so I can see her brown eyes beneath her cap. "She's not going to die, honey. And Rhondi didn't fall that far down. She's going to be okay, too. We just have to get down there and check. And"—I look at the others—"we have to stay calm and connected."

They nod.

"Good," I say. There's no cell reception, so we're on our own. "You know," I offer, "you are the most resourceful girls I've ever met. If I know anything about you, it's that we're going to work this out."

"Should we do GOAL now, Molly?" asks Sophia. She's so levelheaded.

"Good thinking. Now," I say, thinking of G for *Goal*, "what's the goal here?" I answer my own question. "To check on Rhondi. To get her to a safe place.

"O is for *Organize*. Organize a plan." I don't know how, but I remember this. "I'm going to climb down to

Rhondi to make sure she's okay. If for some reason something happens to me, all of you are to start walking back the way you came." I pause and look at each one. "Do you understand? You leave us here and go get help. Don't run. Don't panic. Just follow the trail back, walk down that little hill, and follow the blacktop loop to the forest ranger's station."

They nod. Okay. "Emily?" I say, handing her my phone. "Here's my phone. If you all have to hike out, you keep trying to dial nine-one-one. There might be a signal somewhere, okay?"

She sniffs. Two long ponytails hang down behind her ears and reflect the drawn worry on her face. Under her cape her T-shirt reads GIRL POWER. "You've got it, Em. I trust you, okay? Girl Power." She straightens her shoulders and nods.

"Now I'm going to go down and check on Rhondi."

"What letter is that, Molly?" Sophia's eyes squint in concern.

"It's okay, Sophia. We're just doing stuff out of order, but it's all good." This GOAL thing is what naturally happens when you follow through with a plan. I just realized this tidbit, but reverse for a second to assure the girls that our bases are covered. "Emily taking the phone is *L,* for *Looking Glass.* We're looking ahead at any possible bumps in the road. Now, it's time to *Act. A.*"

"Be careful!" Claire grabs my waist.

"Calm down, Claire," says Emily. "Molly said we need to stay calm."

"That's right, Claire." I tenderly peel Claire off me and pat her shoulder. Her fair skin has her the most pink of all, and along her hairline, her blond hair is moist with sweat. "It'll be okay, honest." I hope I'm right.

Now for the truth. I've got to do this. *A* is for *Action*. I tighten the straps on my backpack and eyeball where Rhondi takes up most of the ledge. The only place to gain footing to go down is in an area with no ledge below. The next hard ledge if I fall is twenty more feet away. I carefully creep down the side of the hill, holding on to some rocks for dear life and fixing my toes into crevices. "Breathe, Molly," I whisper as I guide my foot down a little more, setting off a crumbling cascade of dirt.

About five feet away, I shift my body to the right so that Rhondi is directly underneath me should I fall. Carefully trying not to stomp on her outstretched hand, I wiggle my foot until it gently makes contact with Rhondi's ledge. Safe.

With a shallow turn, I kneel down toward her. "Rhondi?" She doesn't respond. I place my two fingers on the fleshy area beneath her chin and find a pulse. A beating pulse. Louder then, "Rhondi!"

"Is she alive?" Maribel yells down.

"Yes." I can hear their buzzing of relief.

I pull the water bottle from my backpack, gently touch Rhondi's bowling ball–sized head, then trickle water over her flushed face.

Her eyes pop open like she's just sprung out of a dream. Her body's completely still. She groans.

"Rhondi? Can you talk?"

Her mouth opens. "Where are the girls?" The words tumble out of her like they were hard to string together.

"They're fine. You fell and we're going to get you out of here." I have no idea how we're going to do this, but one thing at a time. "Can you move your legs?"

She closes her eyes and groans again.

"How about some water?" I gently tip the bottle to her dry lips and she swallows. "I think your leg is broken. If you move too fast, you could make it worse. We're just gonna go one little bit at a time. Can you move your neck?"

She slowly swivels it back and forth. "Good," I say.

"I have to get up." She tries to lift her torso from the ground.

"No." I gently press her back down. I'm pretty sure she can't bite me in her current state. "You might hurt yourself. Like I said, your leg looks broken. We've got to keep you still. There's no cell phone signal, so we're going to have to go for help. I think it's best if we leave you here while we go for help. There's enough light in the day to get back here before it's too late."

"Okay," she mutters. "Good, Molly." Last night, the thought of her getting eaten alive by a bobcat probably wouldn't have bothered me. But now that it's an actual possibility, I yell up to the girls and five heads look down toward me.

"Girls, I'm going to need your capes." Within seconds, a wave of red satin billows down into my arms and our plan is in action.

31

"C'mon, Molly!" Daddy yells at me from the work truck in the driveway, where he and the entire man-clan wait for me.

I stick my head out my attic window and see streamers of pink clouds in the sky, the afterglow of sunset. "I'll be right down." I take one last glance in the full-length mirror on the back of my bedroom door and center my cape so it's distributed evenly on both shoulders. It's Halloween, but I'm not in costume tonight.

When I reach down to turn off my nightstand lamp, the statuette of Mom wobbles from my quick movement. I felt her inside me yesterday on the trail. Not like I was possessed or heard her ghost speak. No, it was that I didn't doubt myself. Daddy always says Mom was decisive and strong, and while I figured I didn't inherit those traits, I now think they've been with me all along, only I've been too busy doubting myself to notice.

"Molly!" Daddy calls again from outside, and I hightail it down the stairs. I feel bad that he and the uncles worked all weekend but am glad they'll get some time to relax tonight at the Banshee. I rush through the hallway where the Virgin Mother waits with her open arms and pass the familiar faces of the family portrait. Outside the door, a small shiver waves over me. Finally, fall is here, although once you find a weather pattern in Southern California, you can be sure it's going to change.

Uncle Murph, Uncle Rourke, and Uncle Garrett crowd together like sardines in the backseat of the truck. Daddy turns the key and the engine growls. "C'mon, girl," says Granddad, who stands outside the passenger door in his leprechaun suit and waves me into the cab to sit between him and Daddy. Granddad's the only one in costume.

"Sorry to make you guys wait," I say as I strap in.

"Well, you're lucky we like you." Uncle Murph pats my shoulder.

"So," says Daddy, "do you know where this Rhondi woman lives, then?"

"On Oleander." I'm nervous about seeing her, not sure how she's going to react. Dede came by earlier and told me Rhondi was released from the hospital this morning. Strange to think that less than twenty-four

hours ago she was Life Flighted to the hospital by heli-
copter from the Pacific Crest Trail. The girls and I had
to leave Rhondi on the trail, but not without covering
and cushioning her with capes. Once we made it off the
trail, we ran to the forest ranger's station, where they
called 911 and then called parents.

The parents rushed and got to the loop in under an
hour. Ayisha's mom brought Dede, and Dede drove
Claire and me home in Rhondi's white van, which felt
strangely like a privilege.

"What's with the cape?" asks Uncle Garrett from
the backseat. I watch his green sea-glass eyes in the
rearview.

"Dressing for Halloween, are ya?"

"No, it's a Girl Corps thing," I answer.

"You nervous about talking to her?" Daddy asks. I
had filled my family in this afternoon without giving
too much detail about my Friday night.

"A little."

"Well," says Uncle Murph from the back, "you told
us you were gonna apologize. Nothing wrong with
that. Best to do that and leave the bad tale where you
found it."

" 'Sright, Mol." Uncle Rourke taps my shoulder
with his finger. "There's no wise man without a fault."

I turn to face him. "*Woman*, you mean?"

"Of course!" he says.

"You lads stop while you're ahead," says Daddy.
"Just be honest, Mol. Say what you need to say."

Daddy offers me his broad smile. The duel of words between my uncles stops, so I reach out to the black knob on the radio. The dull buzz of the AM signal hums behind an advertisement. I switch to FM and immediately, Uncle Rourke says, "Do you hear that? Thin Lizzy on the radio! Turn it up, Molly girl."

"Hold on to your britches, Rourkey," says Granddad.

I turn up the volume. It's a great song, "Dancing in the Moonlight." It's fast, and the bass, guitar, and drums share the spotlight of the rhythm. Phil Lynott's voice is deep, like Jimi Hendrix but lighter, with more lilt. Daddy taps on the steering wheel and the uncles start a percussion section on the back. Granddad and I sway and snap our fingers until Daddy turns onto Oleander, and the drum section becomes one with my anxious stomach.

Daddy stops the truck in front of the house that bears Rhondi's address. I wonder for a moment if Dede gave me the wrong house number.

Rhondi's yard is lush with greenery, from shrubs to trees to the beautiful blanket of grass. There are about two dozen bird feeders hanging from trees, three lawn gnomes, and a forest full of other shadowed ceramic critters. Most impressive is the bounty of flowers in her yard. Potted and free-roaming, vined and short-stemmed. The fact that they've survived the recent heat is a miracle.

"I'll be quick," I say to Daddy, Granddad, and the uncles, and Granddad bows back into the truck. "You'll come right back, right, Daddy?"

"Yes, love. I'm just gonna drop these fellas off at the Banshee. Won't take me long at all. Don't worry. You have your phone, right?" I nod. "Just go in there and be honest with her," he says.

In the backseat, the uncles nod in support.

As I walk toward the enchanted walkway, the truck rumbles off down the street. I can do this. I know I can. The woman who makes me nervous is the same one who would tell me to put one foot in front of the other. To follow through.

At the front step I'm further encouraged by a welcome mat that actually says WELCOME! Once I push the doorbell, I hear a lengthy, digitized grandfather-clockish gonging sound inside that surprises me, given Rhondi's proven distaste for ring tones.

The door swings open. "Hey," says Michael. Today he's not the man in black, but the man in a cool Beethoven T-shirt.

"Hey, Michael. Is your mom around?"

"Yeah, come on in." We pass red and white plaid upholstered couches in the main room. I'm surprised that the house is so well decorated. There's not a side table without a candlestick or vase, or a wall without a mirror or framed flower print.

He leads me down a short hallway along which a time line of his life covers the walls, from construction-paper artwork done in elementary school to a recent photo of him in a black gown and mortarboard. Rhondi takes such pride in the girls, I guess it follows that she adores her own son.

Michael stops to knock on the door. "Mom?" It's so bizarre to me that her own son calls her Mom, even though it shouldn't be. I haven't really considered Rhondi as a person that much, the same way I've always regarded teachers as if they're creatures who live, eat, and breathe school. It just doesn't follow that they have homes and families and hobbies. "Someone's here to see you."

"Come on in."

The door opens and there lies Rhondi in a tall bed with a novel in her hand and a black cat curled at her feet. "Molly."

"Hi, Rhondi." Michael retreats into the hallway from which we came. I walk closer to the bed and see that without her bejeweled cape, she looks like a movie star caught without makeup, older, with lines and ruddy blemishes. She sits on top of her white eyelet comforter, in generic gray sweatshorts and a black BARRY MANILOW ONE NIGHT LIVE concert shirt that shows a scrawny guy in a white suit who I assume is Barry Manilow himself. Rhondi's toes peek out from a cast that contains her broken leg, which is perched on a tall pile of decorative pillows.

"I'm glad you're here," she says.

"Are you feeling okay?"

"Honestly?" she asks. "I've been better. The doctor said I'll be in this cast for at least six weeks. Good thing Michael can drive and—"

My phone rings. No way. Not now! "I am so sorry." In a panic, I reach in my pocket, feel for the thin button on the side of my phone, and press it for silence.

It's silent now. My phone interrupted. I have no idea who called, but that doesn't matter because I need to say what I came here to say. I force myself to look back at Rhondi. She waits for me to say something, like she knows I have to get it out. "I came here to say I'm sorry, Rhondi."

She doesn't butt in, so I keep talking. "We definitely got off on the wrong foot, and I know it was wrong of me to be late the other night. You were very clear about what time I needed to be there, and I messed up. I just . . ." I suck on my tongue for a moment, a surge of emotion tumbling inside me. "I can't— I need this. I know I'm not the perfect candidate, but I need to see this through." I wipe a tear off my cheek.

"I'm stronger here, with you and the girls. I'm learning this whole other side of me. The Girl Journal even makes me think about myself in new ways." I'm totally bursting out now, but it's honest. "And if it weren't for this group, I think I'd be making choices based on fear, not self. For the first time in my life I'm paying attention to that voice inside me. I don't want to stop hearing it, so I'm asking you, please, to give me a second chance."

Rhondi takes a deep breath. "I am hard on you, I know that, Molly. I expect more from you because you're older and naturally the girls look up to you. But this weekend, you showed up." Her voice lightens, like she's telling me something miraculous. "You came through, Molly. Somehow, you got up to that mountain and you found us. That, my dear, is a hell of a follow-through."

My mother's been gone for so long, I don't know what it would sound like to hear her tell me she's proud, but I'd like to think that this is how I'd feel.

"If you weren't there, I don't know what those girls would have done. You led them, Molly, and I'm proud of you."

"Thank you," I squeak.

"Here." She waves me over to her nightstand, plucks out a tissue, and when she hands it to me, she holds on for a moment and gives me a squeeze. "You did good, Molly. You did good."

I honk out a massive blow of my nose, the tissue crumpling into a soggy ball.

"Now," she says, her tone all business again. "I am going to need you for the Thanksgiving food drive that's coming up. I'll give you all the information on Thursday."

"I'll be there." I jab my thumb toward the door. "I better get going. I'm having dinner with my family tonight."

"Thanks for coming by, Molly."

"Sure," I say, and pivot toward the door.

"Oh, and Molly?"

"Yeah?"

"I like the cape."

"Thanks." Once I'm out of the room, I literally run down the hallway, ready to aim my arms toward the sky and fly.

When Daddy and I walk into the Banshee that night, you'd think Van Morrison himself was onstage, the way the people are dancing to "Spanish Rose," but it's just his amazing voice coming out through the speaker. No one seems to care that it's not live.

In the middle of the hubbub, Uncle Garrett dances with a grateful fiftysomething who's about twelve feet taller than he is.

"Hey there, Molly!" Granddad reaches out for a hug from the booth. I kiss him, then Uncle Rourke.

"Daryl made cheese curds tonight," Aunt Tip says, pushing a plate toward me.

"Looks good," says Daddy, ready to sit down.

"Man, you don't even know," groans Uncle Murph. "They're like little cheese clouds from heaven."

"So?" asks Uncle Rourke. "How'd it go?"

I had told Daddy about the encounter with Rhondi

in the car and break the episode down for the uncles in just a few words: "It went well."

"Let's start playing some music, already!" says Granddad. "We got all night to eat."

"That's fine, Da," says Daddy. "What do you want to play?"

Granddad rattles off a playlist.

"I'll go get Buttons," I say to the men at the table, then turn from them and walk down the hallway toward Aunt Tip's office. It was Nessa who called earlier, while I was with Rhondi. I still need to open her text. Once I'm in Aunt Tip's office, I slip my phone from my pocket, and read the text from Vanessa. YOU GET DOWN THAT MOUNTAIN?

Yes, I got down the mountain, but the reality is, there's always another one to climb on the horizon.

Trevor's not going to disappear, and for all I know, there are more guys like him out there. And seriously, thank God for my family of caring men and the Justin Kubilnickys of the world or I might think *all* guys are card-carrying members of the jackass club.

Still, tomorrow I'll be at school with Trevor. I'm not interested in having to go through the push and pull of the last few weeks. I should take care of this before he has a chance to start calling and texting and barging into my life again. I don't want to have to rehash what I saw at Zach's party in order to stave him off.

I SAW YOU AT ZACH'S WITH ANOTHER GIRL. I'VE MOVED ON, TREVOR. GOODBYE.

My thumb lingers above the Send button.

I'm sure I'll see him and my body will go weak again, when really I should feel the same nausea and disgust I did with yesterday's hangover. I'm human, though. It still hurts to have lost him, to have been cheated on, to know that he said I love you and that I said it back.

I'm not sure what part of the anatomy is responsible for triggering sweaty palms and stomach butterflies, but I do know it's dangerous to completely surrender to those kinds of cues. I guess I'm the kind of person who has to rely more on her head. I may have misread Trevor, but I can't deny there was enough inside me to know that I shouldn't go all the way with him. I don't know what to call that, either. I'm just grateful to have it.

My thumb firmly presses Send, and I place my phone on Aunt Tip's desk. I grab Buttons from his case and head back out toward the pub, where the sound system has been turned off and the stage readied for open mike. The men of my family assemble onstage. "Here she comes!" yells Uncle Murph.

"C'mon, Molly girl!"

I mount the tiny stage. Daddy leans in to me and holds his fiddle beneath his chin. "We're playing 'The Waxies' Dargle.' You got any desire to lead?"

"Absolutely," I say, and without a cue, I start pumping Buttons, the men chime in after the first four bars, and the happy faces of the crowd cheer us on.

Tomorrow I'll go to school and maybe someone will

recognize me as the girl who used to go out with Trevor Shultz, or Vanessa Travere's sidekick, or the girl who puked in Zach Hegel's bathroom.

It won't matter, because up here onstage with my family and my cape, I know who I am at my core.

What kind of girl is at your core?

Find out by creating your own Girl Corps journal and answering these fun and thought-provoking questions.

1. What does it mean to be a girl?

2. What do you like about yourself?

3. What's important to you, and why?

4. In what ways are you different from other people you know?

5. Whom do you admire, and why?

6. What are you good at?

7. Whose friendship do you value most, and why?

8. What is something you'd like to change about yourself, and why?

9. How do you best express yourself? Through art? Writing? Music?

10. What event in your life has affected you the most, and why?

11. What three items would you want with you if you were stranded on a desert island?

12. How would you describe your family?

13. What do you see as your role in your family, and why?

14. What do you think is good about the world?

15. How would you describe the community where you live?

16. What do you have to offer people in need?

17. What kinds of things do you do to take care of yourself?

18. What can you do to be healthier?

19. Should people say what they think even though it might hurt someone's feelings? Why or why not?

20. What stops you from saying what *you* think?

21. What's the most important book you've ever read, and why?

22. Describe how a certain book or movie has made you think about your life differently.

23. What is your favorite subject in school, and why?

24. What does inner strength look like to you?

25. Describe a moment when you exhibited inner strength.

26. Where do you enjoy spending your time, and why?

27. If you could travel the world, where would you go, and why?

28. What concerns you most about the environment?

29. What are you afraid of, and why?

30. Who in your life has had the most impact on you, and why?

31. What's the best advice someone has ever given you? Did you take it?

32. What do you see as your personal motto?

33. What choice you have made in your life has affected you the most?

34. Have you ever gone along with something you didn't want to do? Why or why not?

35. What do you feel you need that you currently don't have?

36. What is something you want to learn about that you feel will make you a better person?

37. Make a list of questions you have. Circle the ones for which you're willing to seek the answers.

38. If your shadow could talk, what would it say to you?

39. Describe a failure in your life and how you recovered.

40. Are you accountable or are you a victim? Explain.

41. Create a collage of yourself using words and pictures.

42. Make a list of everything you know.

43. Make a list of everything you *want* to know.

44. What do you do when you're bored?

45. Describe a memorable dream or nightmare.

46. How do the choices you make now affect your future?

47. What bothers you the most about being a girl?

48. What do you *love* most about being a girl?

49. "Anything boys can do, girls can do better." True or false? Explain.

50. What's been the best day of your life so far? Why?

51. If your clothes could talk, what would they say about you?

52. List at least twenty things you want to do in your lifetime.

53. Describe a friendship you've lost, and explain how it happened.

54. What messages are girls your age given through the media?

55. Complete the following phrases: *I was . . . I am . . . I will be . . .*

56. What do you believe about faith, and why?

57. If you could switch places with anyone for a day, who would it be, and why?

58. What do you miss most about being a young child?

59. Have you ever set a goal and achieved it? Explain.

60. What is one goal you want to achieve within the next few months?

61. Organize your current goal into a statement (*I will . . .*).

62. What are things you need to *do* to achieve your goal?

63. Describe what it will look like when you reach your goal.

64. How will you weigh the success of the goal you've set?

65. In what ways will you celebrate or acknowledge that you have met your goal?

66. Describe a time when something changed for you and you thought it was a negative change but now, looking back, you realize it was positive.

67. Has someone you loved ever changed? If so, how did this change affect your relationship with that person?

68. Has someone ever asked *you* to change? If so, how did you respond?

69. Is it important for you to be accepted by others? Why or why not?

70. Have you ever taken a risk that helped you to grow? Explain.

71. What is a positive risk that you need to take?

72. Write a letter to someone asking for help. When you're finished, write a letter back as if you are the person who is helping you.

73. What is the best thing about being your age?

74. Write a dialogue between you and someone with whom you need to talk. Tell that person everything you might not say to his or her face and have him or her respond to you.

75. Describe yourself, from the top of your head to the bottom of your feet.

76. Write about what you want your life to look like ten years from now—and write it in present tense, as if you were living that life.

77. Write about a time when you felt safe.

78. What makes you laugh, and why?

79. What makes you cry, and why?

80. Write about someone you don't know who fascinates you.

81. Write about a time when you broke the rules.

82. Write a poem or song that describes your current mood.

83. Write about home—what it means to you, what it looks like, how you feel when you're there.

84. Describe the most embarrassing moment you've ever had and how you dealt with it.

85. Write a description of the perfect day, from waking to going to sleep.

86. What is something you would do if you knew no one would judge you for it?

87. Take a piece of paper and fold it down the middle. On the left side, write ten words that describe you; on the right side, write a poem about yourself that incorporates those ten words.

88. How is reality different from what you see on television?

89. Explain one flaw you have that you also consider a strength.

90. What is one question you're afraid to answer?

91. Find a photo you've taken. Look at it for two minutes, and then write down all the emotions that come to mind.

92. What makes you angry?

93. What is something you feel optimistic about?

94. What will you do tomorrow that you didn't do today?

95. What is something you owe someone? How will you repay him or her?

96. When was the last time you felt excited about something? Why?

97. Describe a time when you were hiding from something, and what led you to come out of hiding.

98. What part of the day do you look forward to most, and why?

99. What do you expect from other people?

100. What is something you'd like to learn to accept about yourself?

STACEY GOLDBLATT is the author of *Stray* and a former junior high school English teacher. She lives with her husband, two children, and a dusty accordion in Encinitas, California. Visit her on the Web at www.staceygoldblatt.com.

Can Natalie resist the urge to stray?

STACEY GOLDBLATT

You can't put love on a leash

stray

A NOVEL

Sixteen-year-old, straight-laced, dog-loving Natalie Kaplan compares herself to the Ibizan hound— quiet, loyal, and above all, obedient. But when the hot new intern at her mother's vet clinic comes to live with them for the summer, Natalie's willingness to obey is overcome by her urge to stray.

 www.randomhouse.com/teens RHCB Delacorte Press